Piper didn't have  **wanted to use th** **getting someone** **out to help her, she'd** **have to accept Caleb's offer.**

"I'd appreciate that," she said, swallowing her pride. "I keep my tools over there." She indicated a grey-and-red multidrawer tool chest near the barn entrance.

Piper went and extracted the correct tools. Caleb met her halfway, taking several from her. Their hands touched and she felt the warmth of his palm against hers.

It had been a while since she had that kind of reaction to a man. She reminded herself she wasn't here for romance and that he wasn't here for the long run. Neither was she.

But Piper couldn't ignore this feeling or wanting to get to know Caleb more.

Dear Reader,

You briefly met Caleb Masters in my previous book, *Healing the Doctor's Heart*. I knew from the moment he stepped on the page that Cal would tell me his story, and here it is in *His Montana Star*.

Cal meets our heroine, Piper, a stunt coordinator living on the ranch next to his. Piper has had some troubles in her past and she allowed me to indulge in one of my fantasies—movie stunts. I love movies and I'm fascinated by how the movies make everything look real—explosions, scaling mountains, dangling over the edge of a building, and will we ever forget any of the *Mission Impossible* escapades? Cal, an engineer, suggests they make one of her stunts a reality, not knowing the affect it would have on their relationship and the Hollywood community.

Thank you for joining me as Cal and Piper's adventure unfolds. If you're interested in this and other books I've written, you can contact me at shirleyhailstock.net or on Facebook or Twitter @shailstock.

Thanks again and as always, keep reading.

Shirley Hailstock

Shirley Hailstock began her writing life as a lover of reading. She likes nothing better than to find a quiet corner where she can get lost in a book, explore new worlds and visit places she never expected to see. As an author, she can not only visit those places, but she can be the heroine of her own stories. The author of forty novels and novellas, Shirley has received numerous awards, including a National Readers' Choice Award, a Romance Writers of America's Emma Merritt Award and an *RT Book Reviews* Career Achievement Award. Shirley's books have appeared on several bestseller lists, including the *Glamour*, *Essence* and *Library Journal* lists. She is a past president of Romance Writers of America.

Books by Shirley Hailstock

Harlequin Heartwarming

Summer on Kendall Farm
Promises to Keep
Healing the Doctor's Heart

Visit the Author Profile page
at Harlequin.com for more titles.

To the Harlequin Heartwarming team, especially my editor. They never pushed me to complete my book during the COVID-19 pandemic and its aftermath. Thank you, team. I appreciate your support.

CHAPTER ONE

"HI-YO, SILVER." Piper Logan couldn't help shouting that slogan. She'd done it since her first ride on Silver. Other than family, it reminded her of two things she loved—the ranch and horses. Again, she shouted to the wind as she pulled the reins and clenched her knees.

Her black mare had a silver mane and tail. The horse rose up on strong hind legs and pedaled the air before settling back to earth. Patting the mare's long neck, Piper smiled with pleasure. Leaning forward, she again used her knees to communicate her wishes to Silver, who took off running. The wind tinged Piper's cheeks and snatched her hair away from her face. She loved the feel of the ride, the freedom of being on a horse. In the saddle, she was one with the elements, carefree and exhilarated. Many people sought freedom in the skies, on the open road or by sailing. She attained hers atop a horse. It was a good thing. She'd begun her career because she could handle a horse. And she'd learned to ride here on her aunt and uncle's ranch.

The ranch was hers alone now. Spending so much time in California, Piper had nearly forgotten how she loved being there. In the last year, she'd enjoyed having this place to come to. Solitude and reflection were what she needed, but the nightmares of the accident that brought her from the Hollywood fantasy factory to Waymon Valley, Montana, finally seemed to have abated. She was sure the horseback riding and teaching kept her mind off memories of the past. But when night fell, when the quiet of her thoughts were the only noise in the room, she returned to that movie set and found the tumbling metal replaying in her mind.

Pushing the thought aside, Piper slowed Silver to a trot and then a gentle walk. Sliding down from the saddle, she surveyed the vast landscape. She loved Montana. The day was warm and comfortable. And the mountains in the background added to its beauty. She took in the scenery for a few moments.

A student would arrive in an hour and she wanted to run through one of her routines before she had to cool the horse down and be ready for a basic training class. Routines always made her focus. She needed to be in the moment, concentrating on what she was doing to avoid errors and accidents.

Again she patted Silver's neck and climbed back into her seat. "Let's go, girl," she said, and with the click of her tongue, horse and rider were in the wind.

CALEB MASTERS PACED the floor of his living room. He'd been banned from the kitchen after breakfast by his housekeeper-cook and sometimes surrogate mother, Naomi. He carried a half-full cup of coffee as he walked. Cal's brother, Jake, came to mind. In a way, he envied his only sibling. Not because they were brothers in their thirties and no longer tried to one-up the other for parental attention. And not because Dr. Jake Masters was a world-class surgeon. But because his brother had found the woman of his dreams and he appeared to be happier than Cal ever expected to be. He remembered the way Jake and his bride, Lauren, had looked at their wedding. The love they shared was tangible to anyone who witnessed it.

Cal had no thoughts of being married. Still, he wondered what it would be like to have a woman adore him and he adore her the way his brother and sister-in-law did. It was probably the idleness of him doing little that had him thinking of relationships. It had been a while since he was involved with a woman. Cal's job took him all over the world. Having a wife meant settling in one place, and while he was at his ranch on hiatus, he wasn't planning to stay for longer than a few months. Even that might be cut short since he'd been there for a week and was already itching for something to do. Plus, the only people he'd seen were Naomi, her husband, and a few folks in town.

That was until now.

Cal stepped out onto the porch and squinted to see clearer. He had spotted someone. A woman riding a horse. But as he watched her, she more than rode. She was one with the animal, moving as the horse did, a natural connection between horse and rider. The late afternoon sun shone through her fiery hair as it bounced and fell like a fluttering ribbon of red and gold.

Who was she? Cal wondered. And why was she riding along the ridge of his property? He watched her for a long time. She rode well and he enjoyed seeing the movement of woman and horse. Cal could ride, and seeing her, he wanted to do it again. He was just turning away when she did something unexpected. He froze, his hand on the screen door, staring. His mouth was suddenly dry. She fell off the horse. It was dragging her as she held on to the saddle horn.

Cal was already in motion before he realized he was running. His hands grabbed the porch railing as his body scaled the banister and his boots hit the ground. Coming up from a crouch position, he scanned the ridge, looking for her. He spotted her just as she righted herself, using her own momentum to swing back into the saddle.

"What?" he asked no one. Was she some sort of contortionist? He'd clearly seen her fall. Yet, as he continued to watch, she jumped down, even though the horse didn't slow by a millisecond, took a couple of running steps in unison with the animal and then, defying gravity and the laws of physics, used acrobatic tricks to retake her seat.

Cal's mouth dropped open. Raising a hand, he shielded his eyes, following her progress. "What is she doing?" Again his question was directed to no one. Cal was mesmerized by her ability. She was an expert. She knew exactly how and when to drop from the seat and when to pull herself back into place. He marveled at her power and strength. Who was she? he wondered again. And where had she learned to ride like that? He could ride. He'd done it since he was a child, but her acrobatics were way beyond anything he'd ever done or thought of doing.

"Cal? Cal, where are you?"

He looked up. Naomi stood on the porch. With her hands settling on her ample hips, she searched right and left, before spying him.

"What are you doing over there?" she asked as she reached the porch's edge. "Oh, I see," she said flatly, her eyes trained on the ridge. "Your lunch is ready."

"Who is that?" Cal asked, ignoring Naomi's words and hooking his head toward the horse and rider.

Squinting, Naomi continued to look in the direction he indicated. She smiled, something she didn't often do.

"That's Piper Logan. She's running that place now. Hadn't been around in years, but for the last twelve months she's been over there full-time. Teaches horseback riding to the kids from town. Keeps your horses, too."

Cal could see why. "She's excellent with a horse."

"Always has been," Naomi acknowledged. "From what I hear, she did some trick riding in Hollywood. Got a job doing it, too."

Cal knew Naomi knew more than that. Despite the short time he'd been at the ranch, he'd learned that she was a force in the Valley and that she knew all there was to know. Yet she didn't volunteer much. Not a gossip, Cal thought. But at this moment, he wanted more details about the woman on the ridge.

"Why is she back here?" he asked. "Hollywood sounds fascinating." Cal had been to enough places to admit that some people liked the pace of a big city and others enjoyed the quiet solitude of a small town.

"Don't know," Naomi said. "She's not

much for talking these days. You'd better come in before your lunch gets cold."

Cal hesitated for several seconds. He knew that was Naomi's way of saying the subject was closed. He didn't want to leave. Piper's ability mesmerized him. However, he eventually heeded Naomi's warning and went inside, but looking over his shoulder all the way to the door. He ate quietly and alone. Naomi was a great cook and he was lucky that she and her Jack-of-all-trades husband took care of the place. He'd inherited her services from the previous owner, and while he'd only been in Montana a few times, he considered Naomi a friend.

Pushing his plate aside, Cal stood up and took it to the kitchen. He fended for himself for his evening meal, although she often left something in the refrigerator for him to heat up later if he wasn't there at dinnertime.

"Do you have any more of that cake from yesterday?" he asked, setting the plate in the sink and running water to clean away the remnants.

"I'll cut you a slice."

"I'd like two slices."

She turned and looked at him.

"And could you put them in a takeaway dish?"

Naomi stood up to her full height and looked at him. "You're going to meet her," she stated.

"It's the neighborly thing to do," he said, hiding a smile.

"Good luck with that." She frowned.

Cal raised his brows, questioning her comment.

"She's a little reclusive, doesn't open up easily to new people," Naomi said. "She hasn't spent much time reacquainting herself with the neighbors."

Cal looked through the window. Piper was his nearest neighbor. Out here, the word *neighbor* was a loose term. It could mean as far away as twenty miles.

"I'll appeal to her horse sense," he told his housekeeper, who gave him a cynical look, then turned to cut the cake.

With the two slices in hand, Cal left in the wake of Naomi's laughter. Piper had been riding a horse, but he chose to drive. Minutes later he climbed out of the cab of his Dodge Ram and went up the steps to her front door. She didn't answer the doorbell after two tries. Hearing the clopping of horse hooves, he walked to the side of the porch. Her stables were set away from the main house and she was teaching. He waited for her to finish as she patiently taught her student the basics of sitting in a saddle and adjusting to the rhythm of movement.

Once the child was picked up, Piper handed her horse off to a groom, who took the reins.

Cal approached the stables. As she spoke briefly to the groom, Piper gave no sign that she had seen Cal walk up.

"Hello," Cal said, from behind her.

She left the groom at the sound of his voice. The man led the horse away and Piper stepped toward Cal.

"Caleb Masters," he said, extending his hand.

"So you're the new person at the Christensen place," she said. She didn't shake his hand or stop to greet him but continued walking toward the house. "About time you came to inspect the property."

"I've been here before. I didn't buy it sight unseen. And it's no longer the Christensen place."

Ignoring his last comment, she said, "Well, I've been here for a year and this is the first I've heard of you being in residence. If you've stopped by to see your horses, they're in the stable. I'll have time to show you the way tomorrow."

"Oh, right. My horses," Cal repeated.

"Didn't you know?" She squinted at him but kept walking.

"They were already boarded when I returned here," he told her. "Since they need exercise and you already had permission to use them, even for the students, I let them stay where they were."

"Well, now you know they're in that barn." She pointed toward the building where the groom had taken her training horse. "I suppose you'll be moving them soon."

"Only if that's a problem."

"It isn't," she said. "We've been boarding horses for years. And I've been told your stay here is temporary. They will need a home when you're gone."

So she knew about him. He wondered who she'd talked to. It sounded as if she was already dismissing him. Naomi had warned him she was reclusive.

"I bought the ranch as an investment. I'm an engineer. My last job shut down without notice." He stopped. Cal wasn't going into details about the closure. "Usually, I'd go to New York, but my brother got married last year and it was a little *inconvenient*."

"I see I'm not the only newcomer. From what I hear, you haven't been around that long, either."

She stopped then and turned to him. "What have you heard?"

Her voice was strong. It was almost an accusation or a command. Cal was taken aback. "Not much. Only that you've been here a year and you teach riding," he explained. But he wondered why she was so defensive.

She said nothing, only stared at him a long moment before turning and resuming her walk.

"Could you stop a moment? I only wanted to be neighborly."

She stopped.

"I brought you a dessert. It's what people used to do to be friendly. I'm not sure if that's still the truth, but that's what I was taught."

He offered one slice of the cake to her.

Piper took it, looking through the clear plastic container. "Dessert," she said. "Cake?"

He nodded.

"I don't eat a lot of carbs." She pushed the container back into his hands.

Cal gave her the once-over. She was wearing black riding pants and boots with a white short-sleeved shirt that was tucked into her pants. He thought she could use a few carbs.

Her hair was redder up close than it seemed when he'd first seen her riding along the ridge. Then the sun had turned it fiery red. Now he saw it was dark red with sprinkles of copper threaded through. She was a head shorter than he was, even though the ground they stood on put her at even height.

"Come on, it's cake," he said. "A very good cake, I might add."

"Did you bake it?"

"I could have. But I didn't. Naomi baked this and she's legendary for her kitchen skills." Cal didn't know this for sure, but from the meals she'd cooked him so far, she was better than good.

"I thought since we're neighbors, you'd offer me some coffee and we could eat the cake together."

"That's not going to happen. Since you've heard about me, you know I'm a loner. I don't do coffee and cake."

She turned again, this time going up the steps to her front door. Cal wondered if she was seeking sanctuary. Why would someone be so unfriendly, especially in Waymon Valley, where every time he stepped out of his truck, someone waved, smiled at him or said hello?

"I see," he said. "If you change your mind, enjoy the cake. Both pieces. And be neighborly and return the containers."

He slipped the two pieces of cake through the porch railings. Piper skipped up the steps and went through the door without giving him a backward glance.

Cal smiled and shook his head as he reached his truck. He opened the door and climbed into the cab. Naomi had been right. Piper Logan was a hard nut to crack, but Cal had dealt with others just as hard, if not harder. Glancing at the twin containers still sitting on the porch, he thought anyone that resistant to friendship probably curled up at night with a large bowl of ice cream and a tearjerker movie. He'd done it with a keg of beer and a revolving door at the pizza shop.

He smiled again. He should have brought her ice cream, but carbs or not, he was sure she'd eventually pick up the dessert.

CAKE, THAT WAS a new one. Piper was still thinking about Cal's unique approach the next day after her lesson as she ran up the stairs to her bedroom. She hadn't heard much about Caleb Masters. Her conversations with the townspeople centered on riding lessons, horse upkeep and the weather. Yet news of the new owner of the Christensen ranch had reached her ears. And he had the nerve to bring her cake. Obviously, he didn't understand that the camera added pounds to a person's image.

Piper stopped in the process of removing her trousers. Of course he didn't. He wasn't part of the industry. In her world, the only people she knew were part of the dream factory. They made movies, supplied fantasies, worked behind the scenes so theatergoers could have a thrilling experience.

Throwing the trousers in the closet, but missing the hamper, she didn't understand why she was so angry. Caleb said he was being neighborly. Maybe it was the entire situation that had forced her to leave Hollywood and return to the ranch. She loved it here, but she didn't want to be here feeling like she'd been run out of Hollywood.

And there was what she'd heard on the news this morning. Her coffee had gone cold in her mouth as Xavier's face on the screen left her with a sour taste. Apparently, he'd completed the large contract she'd begun. Invariably, the segment ended with his association to her. Would she ever live that frightful day down?

Shaking her head at the image that accused her in the mirror, Piper knew she needed some exercise, someplace to expend her pent-up energy. She'd already ridden Silver, but she still felt the need to push her body. Quickly, she changed into her leotard and slipped her feet into a pair of well-worn sneakers. Grabbing her soft sole gymnastic shoes, she left by the back door and headed for the old barn that she'd converted into a personal gym. Entering the cavernous space always made her feel better. Anger slipped from her shoulders. Changing from her sneakers to the beam shoes, she went through the routine of stretching her muscles. With all the teaching she did, the walking and riding, the demonstrations, she should be all right to do some tumbling. Yet she knew how easy it was to injure herself, so she took precautions.

Completing the routine she'd learned years ago, she chalked her hands and saluted the beam. It was the first apparatus she'd trained on and she still went there whenever she practiced. But today she needed something more strenuous. Running across the padded floor, she did several front flips and back flips before coming to a standstill at the other side of the mat. Gathering her hair and pulling it into a ponytail, she secured it. Then repeating the routine, she did flip after flip until she was back at her starting position.

She felt better. The exercise had already begun to glisten her skin. Her muscles were relaxed and ready for what she needed to do. The uneven parallel bars stood before her. Lifting her heels, she went up on practiced legs. Taking a long breath, she ran forward, her speed increasing with each slap of her foot on the mat. Her hands caught the lower bar and she swung her body up. As she came down, her hands and feet were on the same bar ready to swing to the higher one.

Something was wrong. She felt it in the bar's tension.

Stopping her swing, she walked across the mats, checking the connections.

"Hello."

Piper stiffened. The voice came from behind her, but she recognized the deep tone of her new and annoying neighbor.

"What are you doing here?" she asked, spinning around to face him.

"This time I did come to see the horses."

He looked past her at the equipment she'd been checking.

"What are you doing?"

"My plan was to exercise, but I felt something that didn't feel secure."

Without asking first, Caleb Masters came right into the converted barn and started to examine the connections.

"This is not completely secure," Caleb said. Moving past her, he went to the bars and began inspecting the guy cables that attached to the floor and stabilized the setup. Piper followed him.

"I know," Piper responded. "I was about to fix it."

The gym was a converted barn. The outside walls that were once only bare beams and slatted wood had been insulated and closed against the weather. Windows were cut in the sides and skylights adorned the ceiling. The place was bright, and from the inside, there was little evidence that a barn had ever stood in the same place.

Testing each guy-wire cable individually, Caleb paused after an unexpected sound. "This is the one."

Piper pulled the mat that was covering the attachment and found the problem.

"It's the swivel anchor. It's coming up from the floor," she said, hearing the wonder in her own voice.

"And I think this cable tightener is on backward," Caleb said.

"It's facing the wrong way. How could I not notice that?" Piper spoke more to herself than to Caleb. She looked up. "It'll have to be broken down and redone."

"It won't take that long to redo." He glanced up at her. "If you have the tools, I can help."

Piper didn't have a choice. This was a

two-person operation, and if she wanted to use the equipment without getting someone out to help her, she'd have to accept Caleb's offer.

"I'd appreciate that," she said, swallowing her pride. "I keep my tools in that chest." She indicated a gray-and-red multi-drawer tool chest in a corner near the entrance.

Piper went to it, opening various drawers and extracting the correct tools. Caleb met her halfway and took several of them from her. Their hands touched and she felt the warmth of his palm against hers. Dropping her gaze to their hands, she could still feel the heat even though they no longer made contact. It had been a while since she had that reaction to a man. She reminded herself she was not here for romance. He wasn't here for the long run and neither was she. They'd both be going back to their other lives. Piper wasn't sure when she would leave. No one in Hollywood was calling her. Xavier had made sure of that. Pushing thoughts of her ex-fiancé out of her mind, she concentrated on fixing the cables.

Caleb completed his side of the bars before Piper had hers done.

"You're no novice at this," she stated.

"I've put together one or two in my time," he said.

"Really? When? Why?" Piper looked at Caleb, but he was busy with the guy-wires.

"I once worked in a gym."

He didn't add anything further and she didn't pursue the issue. She felt he didn't want to tell her any more and she knew everyone had secrets they'd rather not have exposed. Yet he didn't strike her as aloof. He had an air of...something, she thought, but couldn't define.

They worked in silence until all the bars, tubes and cables were lying on the floor in order.

Piper stood up straight and looked at the arrangement. Everything was in place. All they needed to do was to reassemble it. She glanced at Caleb. He was tall, at least six feet, maybe a little more. By the deepness of his tan, it looked as if he spent a lot of time outside, not only at a job, but also working out. If there was an ounce of fat on him, she didn't know where he was hiding it. His eyes were dark brown, darker than his hair, which had lighter highlights and tended to spike. It seemed darker in the gym than it had outside, but the skylights revealed several changes of color. With powerful legs, broad shoulders, a strong square jawline and a killer smile, he could test for the leading man role at any Hollywood studio.

Piper considered herself lucky that she was immune to Hollywood types. She'd worked with enough of them to know that a lot of them believed their hype.

"Ready to put it together again?" Caleb asked.

It took a breath for Caleb's words to register. "Oh, sure."

She reached down and picked up one of the side tubes. Then realizing her mistake, she put it down again. Caleb said nothing and Piper was grateful for that. Why had she done that? She could put this apparatus together in her sleep. She just hadn't done it in a while. In less than half an hour, the two of them were done.

Caleb tested the bars, first hanging from the higher one and bending his knees to swing. The tension was good, Piper observed, failing to keep her eyes off the lean lines of Caleb's body. On the lower bar, he jumped up and balanced himself on strong thighs. With his back hollowed, his position morphed into a tight arch. He was not a novice, Piper thought. Far from it. She watched him swing fully over the bar before landing on his feet and standing up.

Piper let out a breath as if she'd completed a routine.

"These are not regulation size," Caleb said, looking from the bars to her.

It took her a second to follow what he meant. "I had them custom made because of my height."

She watched as Caleb's eyes took in her frame. He nodded slightly, but it wasn't to her. It felt more like an appraisal, a compliment. She pressed her lips together to keep from smiling.

"Why don't you give it a try?" he said after collecting all the tools and giving her room to pass him.

Piper suddenly felt self-conscious. She'd performed for ten years in front of a full complement of camera operators, actors, directors, grips, carpenters and scores of other people without a second thought. But now, with an audience of one, she felt as if this was an Olympic competition and her entire career depended on her winning.

Taking a long breath, Piper chalked her hands and pulled on her grips. Stepping onto the mat, she raised and lowered her arms, then started her run. Catching the lower bar, she immediately swung into a Stalder position, swinging around the bar several times before piking and transferring to the higher bar. There she swung through several giants before standing still for a beat at the top and turning totally around, reversing her swing.

Dismounting, she felt flushed and hot. The apparatus was strong and safe. "It feels good," she said, still self-conscious. She wasn't a performer. She wanted to thank Caleb and have him return to his ranch. "Thank you for your help."

Caleb didn't immediately move. In fact, he stopped in his tracks. "You're not used to having people help you, are you?"

"I wouldn't say that." She glanced at the bars. "You just helped me put this together."

"But if you could have done it alone, you'd have dismissed me in a moment."

"I thought you were here to see your horses," she said.

"There's no harm in accepting help."

She ignored his comment.

"I don't expect anything in return. It was just a simple act of friendship," Caleb continued.

With that, he closed the drawer of the tool chest and walked through the open doorway. Piper wanted to call him back and explain, but she stopped herself. It was none of his business. He'd volunteered to help correct the configuration of the bars. She had not asked him to. She could also have found the problem herself, but that might have been when it was too late. But she had thanked him. So what was the problem?

Naomi's grin was wide and toothy when Cal came in. "Is that a beer expression or a Johnnie Walker Red?" she asked.

"Black," Cal replied, even though it was nowhere near happy hour.

Naomi laughed again. "At least she didn't throw you out. You were gone a couple of hours."

"I was helping her resecure some gym equipment. The minute it was ready for use, she dismissed me."

Naomi howled, handing him a glass containing a finger of whiskey.

"It's not that funny," Cal said, already beginning to laugh himself.

"That'll teach you."

"Teach me what?" He took a sip from the glass. The liquor was cold, undiluted by anything except three ice cubes. It went down smooth and spread heat throughout his chest.

"Not to mess with Ms. Hollywood."

Cal had learned that Naomi could be a bit caustic, but it was all bravado.

She stretched the syllables out on *Hollywood*, lowering her voice and holding on to the end of the word for three beats longer than necessary.

"Is that what they call her?" He referred to the townspeople, not wanting to single Naomi out. He knew that Naomi would know, and that if asked for information, you got it—straight.

Maybe he would ask about Piper sometime, but not today.

Cal wondered what they called him. People talked in small towns, especially about newcomers. Naomi would tell him if he asked, but he decided not to. Not until he proved himself. And so far, he hadn't proved anything in Waymon Valley. He glanced at the wall toward Piper's ranch. He'd shown her that he could put together a piece of gymnastic equipment, but that hadn't impressed her. She could do it herself, but it would be easier and quicker with help from one of the ranch hands.

"For a few moments I thought she was being friendly." Cal's comment was mostly to himself, yet Naomi stopped stirring something in a bowl.

"You're not the only man who's tried to get her attention."

"It isn't that. I mean I'm not interested in a relationship. It's just that we live next door to each other…"

Naomi was already nodding her head. The gesture said agreement, but her expression was the direct opposite. "This is Montana, Cal. Next door is like twenty miles away."

It wasn't that far, but close to it when you took the main roads. On horseback, it was much closer. And he had noticed an unpaved track that connected his ranch to hers. Yet Cal didn't argue with Naomi. He sort of identified with Piper. Both were outsiders.

Although she seemed a bit unhappy being a recluse. He'd seen his brother bury his feelings and avoid all contact after an accident. Piper had similar tendencies.

He shouldn't interfere in her life. He wasn't staying in Waymon Valley. But his curiosity was piqued. He wanted to know why she shunned friendship.

CHAPTER TWO

ICED TEA, Piper thought. It was her panacea. Whenever the world crowded in on her, and that had been a lot lately, she'd make tea. It was something she'd learned from her mother. Not the actual brewing of the tea, but the calming effect the effort of making it had on her.

The kitchen was huge and comfortable. Her aunt and uncle had owned the place before she inherited it and her aunt had upgraded the kitchen with every modern convenience there was. Yet the room still held the warmth and charm of a country farmhouse.

After pouring herself a tall glass, Piper settled on the cushions under the wall of windows that looked out on the mountains in the distance. As a child, she lived closer to town, but most of her days were spent with her aunt and uncle. She'd sit in the window and read while her aunt baked bread or prepared dinner. She smiled, sipping her tea and remembering her aunt and uncle's efficient movements about the room. There were times when the two would dance across the floor. They really loved each other, and while the memory warmed her, Piper missed them terribly.

She missed the Christensens, too. They had moved to Arizona when Mr. Christensen developed COPD, chronic obstructive pulmonary disease. Two of their three daughters lived in Tucson. Their son moved to Los Angeles. Only Anna, the oldest, remained in the state. After generations of Christensens living on the ranch, they'd sold it to Caleb.

Piper would keep the place as a loving sanctuary. The thousand-acre spread had been a cattle ranch originally, but today it had meadows and horses.

She hadn't been in the Christensen house since she moved away ten years ago. She knew a few people who'd remained in the Valley, and she remembered it as a friendly place. It hadn't changed.

She had.

It was the accident in Hollywood that plagued her. Piper thought that after a year, she'd have forgotten it. But as she'd learned, life rarely followed a set course.

Piper rested the glass of iced tea against her forehead. What was she going to do? She couldn't let Xavier's comments control her life. She'd gone over that stunt at least twenty times before the filming started. Every detail was correct. Every practice was perfect. She knew every inch of the scaffolding well enough that she could put it together blindfolded. She had a recording of the accident. She'd seen it a thousand times. That day was imprinted on her brain. She could recall it as clearly as she remembered what the Montana Rockies look like from astride her horse.

Piper leaned back. She'd never been badly hurt during a stunt. Her injuries were always minor, never requiring a trip to the emergency room. She didn't even have a scratch to point to as a badge of honor.

Piper was meticulous in designing and working out the plans for the director. That was why Xavier had given her the responsibility for the action sequence that proved her downfall. Even though Xavier had checked the rigging and given his approval, Austin, the stuntman, was critically injured and nearly died. News spread like a gasoline fire across Hollywood and the media. Some outlets cast her as incompetent. She was the villain in a production led by sound bites straight from Xavier's mouth. So much for loyalty or support. She was out there on her own, virtually hung out to dry by everyone.

Piper drank the last of the tea. Maybe she should go back and do more exercises, she thought. It hadn't worked its usual magic. Then she thought of Caleb. She'd tried to push him away like she'd done most of the men who showed interest in her. Caleb's actions were friendly, but she knew life would not remain that uncomplicated. Better to cut off any possibility of a future relationship.

The parallel bars in the gym came to mind. She was grateful that Caleb had helped her, even more grateful that he'd seen there was a problem. After never having suffered an injury on the job, she didn't want to fall off her own equipment while she was alone in the gym. Speaking dismissively to Caleb had been a mistake. She thanked him, then showed him the door in practically the same breath. He wasn't Xavier. She knew that, but in that instance he reminded her of him. Not by his looks, but by how he commanded things. How could she have ever thought she and Xavier could make a life together?

Piper got up to clear away the dishes but heard a vehicle coming. Her shoulders dropped. She wasn't ready for Caleb Masters again. But it wasn't Caleb's truck that came to a stop in front of the house.

"Meghan," Piper called, going through the door and rushing down the steps as her friend jumped from the seat of her truck's cab.

Piper and Meghan had known each other since kindergarten and having a friend who always supported her was one of the reasons Piper returned to the ranch.

The two women hugged. Meghan owned a hotel in town and lived in the house attached.

"What are you doing here?"

"I had to go pick up an order in Butte." She hunched her shoulders. "The joys of hotel management. So, as I was out this way, I decided to drop in and see my best friend."

They both smiled and went into the house, naturally stopping in the kitchen. It was their favorite place. Piper poured two cups of coffee, Meghan's preference, and they settled across from each other at the table.

"I'm glad you had time to stop by," Piper said.

"Everything okay?"

"Fine. Except for the kids I give lessons to, I rarely see anyone."

"You could change that."

Piper frowned. She knew she could be more involved in town, but she didn't want to answer all the unasked questions.

"I guess it can be pretty lonely out here with your aunt and uncle gone. I sure miss them."

"I do, too. But I keep busy with the riding school."

"What about *him*? Have you seen him yet?" Meghan asked.

"Him being…" Piper left the sentence hanging.

"Him being the new owner of the Christensen ranch." Meghan glanced in the direction of Caleb's property.

"You mean the Masters ranch," Piper corrected. "Mr. Caleb Masters informed me of that detail himself."

"Ah, so you have met him." Meghan's face lit up. "What's he like? Everyone in town is all abuzz about him."

Meghan was more excited about Piper's neighbor than she was. But then Piper was off men and Meghan was always on the hunt.

"He's a man. You'd like him. He's tall, fit, rugged."

"As in ruggedly handsome?" Meghan smiled.

"If you like that type," she said, smiling.

Meghan flashed her eyes at Piper. "You like him," she stated.

"Not me." Piper put her hands up, palms out, and leaned back as if something awful was about to touch her. "I'm done with men."

"You're not going to let what happened with Xavier turn you away from romance forever, are you?" Meghan's voice was dead serious.

"Not entirely. I'm not ready for a relationship," Piper admitted.

"Okay, but you shouldn't hide yourself away, either. You don't come to town unless absolutely necessary. You don't attend any events, or talk to other people. Only the parents and kids you teach get your warmth. The rest of us are shut out."

"The kids are doing fine." Some were enthusiastic to begin. Others a little apprehensive of such a huge animal, but after their first lesson, all their fears were gone.

"I know they are. Their parents are proud of their accomplishments and think you're an excellent teacher, but they wish you were more sociable."

Piper said nothing. She thought about what Meghan said, but she didn't want to go into town. Invariably, people would want to know about the accident and someone would surely bring up the fact that it was her fault.

"What does that mean? Most of the people we went to school with have moved away."

"So, make some new friends."

"I will," Piper agreed, but she had no intention of doing so. "But not yet."

"I tell you what. There's a new movie in

town I've been dying to see. Why don't you come with me?"

"With you and who?"

"Travis and me, and if you want to bring someone—" Meghan glanced at the wall toward the Masters ranch.

Piper held her hand up to stop her friend. Travis was Meghan's on and off boyfriend. Piper didn't want to be the third person on a date.

"No, thank you. I have plenty to do and I'm not up for a date night or a blind date." There was a clear warning in Piper's tone.

Meghan took a sip of her coffee. She was obviously disappointed.

"All right, how about just lunch with me in the hotel restaurant? At least change your scenery to something different from the sky and the mountains. Being alone all the time is not good for you."

Piper hesitated. She wasn't alone. There were grooms and caretakers on the property. The vet visited, too, from time to time. Still, she knew if she didn't agree to something, Meghan would continue making suggestions until she did.

"All right, lunch."

"Tuesday at one," Meghan prompted.

Piper shook her head. Tuesday was only a few days away. "How about a week from Tuesday?"

"Great," Meghan said, evidently satisfied with the compromise.

Standing up, Meghan said, "I'd better get back now. The hotel would fall apart without me."

Smiling, Piper walked her to the door. She watched as Meghan skipped down the steps and went to her truck. Opening the door, she stopped and turned. She wasn't looking at Piper, but at the distant house that once belonged to the Christensens and now had a completely different resident.

Piper followed her gaze. She felt compelled to do so, as if Caleb Masters knew she was spying on him.

Meghan got behind the wheel. "Next Tuesday," she called as she backed away from the house. "I won't allow a no-show for anything other than hospitalization or death."

Both women smiled and waved. Piper waited until Meghan's truck rounded the bend in the road and all she saw was a cloud of dust. Opening the screened door, she went inside already thinking of a reason to avoid lunch. The last thing she needed was to sit in a crowded restaurant among whispers and stares, even with a friend she'd known since childhood.

CAL LEFT HIS truck in the supermarket parking lot. Walking to the door, he was stopped by several people who greeted him warmly and welcomed him to Waymon Valley. It was a friendly place and he felt buying the ranch as an investment was a good idea, but he'd been in the Valley for over a month and people still greeted him as if he'd arrived yesterday. He supposed it was small-town life. Traveling so much, Cal had experienced different kinds of receptions in the past, some not always good, but he'd have to get used to the overly friendly citizens of the Valley. That is, overly friendly minus one.

Grabbing a cart, he started down the aisles. Naomi usually did the shopping, but Cal needed something to do and he'd offered to run into town and get supplies. Used to heading up a crew and being active as an engineer, Cal was going stir-crazy sitting around doing nothing. His brightest spot had been with his antisocial neighbor, Piper Logan. She had a pretty name and it extended to her features: tall, with dark red hair and highlights that made it glow in the sunlight as fiery as her temperament. Her body was lithe and toned. She had warm brown eyes, and when she smiled, it was winning. By far, her eyes were her best feature, large with depths that seemed to bore into the soul.

And the way she rode a horse. Cal shook his head in appreciation, remembering her on the ridge. It was like nothing he'd ever seen outside of an old movie, but Piper performed as if she and the horse had melded into one.

Pulling his attention back to the store, he took out the list Naomi had given him and went down aisle after aisle pulling the items she'd outlined. The cart filled up quickly, not only with what Naomi needed, but Cal had his own ideas and made his selections accordingly. He'd fended for himself plenty of times, and when Naomi wasn't there, he could whip up a quick meal or set a delectable spread with only an open grill and a handful of ingredients. He recalled several times when he was on a jobsite and the smell of cooking meat sparked an impromptu picnic. His mouth watered at the memories. It had him adding sausage and pork ribs to his cart.

Passing the bakery section, he remembered the cakes he'd left for Piper. A smile tilted the corners of his mouth. He wondered if she'd eaten them. Probably, he concluded. Even though his time in the Valley had been short, he'd heard that no one turned down Naomi's cooking. Rejecting the idea of purchasing pastry, he headed for the cashier. That was when he saw *her*. Cal blinked, making sure it wasn't his imagination conjuring up his thoughts. Piper stood in the frozen foods aisle. She was looking into one of the freezer compartments as if she was deciding what to choose.

He turned away before she could see him. The line at the cashier was long, so he used the self-checkout and was on his way to the exit when he saw a flyer on the wall among business cards and one-page flyers offering services. The photo of a horse grabbed his attention and he stopped. Reading it, he discovered it was Piper's advertisement for horseback riding lessons. While it was directed mainly at kids' lessons, the thought that entered Cal's mind ballooned into a full-blown idea.

In the open air and to no one in particular, he laughed out loud at what he thought Piper's expression would be when she saw his name on an application.

Leaving the market, Cal pushed his cart to the truck and began loading the groceries in the back. He kept his eyes on the door of the store, waiting for Piper to appear. As he put the last bag in the cargo bed, she came out pushing a heavy cart and balancing a bag in her right hand. Cal rushed over.

"Here, let me help you." He took the bag from her before she could refuse.

"What are you doing here?" she asked, looking up at him. "It seems every time I turn around, there you are."

Caleb noticed her eyes. The sunlight made them brighter. Like her hair, they mesmerized him. For a long moment he said nothing.

"Cal?" Piper called.

"A man's gotta eat." He said the first thing that came to mind.

She glanced at him and almost smiled, then pushed the cart toward her truck. "But I thought Naomi did the shopping."

"She was busy this morning and I needed something to do."

"I take it sitting around relaxing doesn't fit your lifestyle?"

"I've been working since I graduated from college. Sitting around and watching the grass grow is a little foreign to me."

"You could always take up a hobby. I hear golfing at the country club is popular."

"Funny you should mention hobbies."

They reached her truck and she swung a bag over the side, settling it on the bottom of the bed near the cab. Cal followed suit.

"I saw your horseback riding notice in the store," he said. "Do you teach adults?"

She stopped, holding a plastic-coated re-usable bag with a long, unwrapped stick loaf of bread poking out of the top. "I haven't done so while I've been here, but I can. Why?"

"I want to enroll."

"What?" She took a step back, cutting her eyes at him as if he'd proposed the worst idea imaginable. "Are you serious?"

Cal watched her expression. He thought she was wondering if he was being facetious.

"I saw you riding. Would you teach me to do some of those tricks?"

Her face changed. Frown lines formed between her eyes. "You don't just get on a horse and try that," she said. "Stunts are an art and they are not learned overnight or during a ten-week session with someone who's only a weekend rider."

Heaving the last bag into the cargo bed, she faced him straight on. "Kids are one thing. They want to learn and many of them are just afraid enough of an animal that size to do what you tell them. Adults are a different story. If you want riding lessons, that's one thing. Stunts and tricks, I don't teach."

Cal was stunned at her abrupt change of attitude. "Why is that? You had to learn them someplace. Wouldn't it be safer to train a person the right way?"

He knew the answer to that. He'd used the technique many times in his career as an engineer, especially when he encountered someone who was resistant to change. He didn't have that impression of Piper. Yet there was something about her that he felt she was hiding. From what he'd heard of her, she was just short of being reclusive. And her attitude seemed to prove it.

"I'll sign a waiver," he prompted, flashing her a wide smile. Cal knew a waiver was part of any sports training arrangement.

"I'm afraid I don't have time for that. Maybe you can check with other riding instructors. Good afternoon."

Without giving him time for an additional argument, she slipped into the driver's seat and started the engine.

Cal walked to the window. "Call me Cal," he said. "We are neighbors."

"Cal," she repeated. "Good luck."

IT WAS NOON the next day before Piper got to her breakfast. She had three back-to-back lessons, but she was free the rest of the day. Curled up in the kitchen window, she savored her second cup of coffee as she watched the calming mountains in the distance. She'd go for a ride later. Maybe head up into the hills, taking her camera and capturing some of the natural beauty of the area. She wasn't a filmmaker, but she'd worked in the industry long enough to have some of the tinsel enter her core.

A beeping noise caught her attention. It came from her office computer. She usually worked her horse riding business in the morning before any lessons, but today she'd overslept. Her night had been marred by thoughts of the accident. Only this time there was a difference. Instead of the jib, or working arm of the crane she'd seen in past dreams, this time there was a parallel gymnastics bar. Chalking it up to thoughts of Cal helping her reset the bars, she tried to push the thoughts aside.

The beeping continued. Usually there was nothing new. Most of the applications for horseback riding lessons had already come in. But there was an occasional one or two a month from people discovering her and sending an inquiry.

Piper had set the machine to notify her of different types of requests. What she heard wasn't a general inquiry. It was an application coming in. She wasn't a computer wizard. But her automatic reply said she'd respond within twenty-four hours, although she usually did it in less time.

Taking her coffee cup, she unwound her

legs from the window seat and headed to the small room off the kitchen that she used as an office.

He didn't. Piper plopped into the chair in front of the screen. She stared at the display for several seconds before blinking. Then she blinked again. Surely she wasn't seeing clearly. Opening her eyes, the screen hadn't changed. Caleb Masters's application for riding lessons was clearly visible. Did he really want lessons or was this another attempt to poke and prod at her?

Piper shook her head, going back to the computer screen. She recalled the first time she'd seen him, the first time they'd touched. And then there was the supermarket. Despite their conversation, she had seen the interest in his eyes. She had hidden her own. Piper didn't trust men. She'd been burned by more guys than just Xavier, although he was the latest. Sadly, it had started with her parents, who ignored her and her siblings in favor of pursuing their careers in the theater and on the silver screen. Even though her aunt and uncle had welcomed them as children and treated them as if they were their own, she'd never quite pushed off the blanket of feeling rejected.

Hunching her shoulders, Piper decided to give her neighbor the benefit of the doubt. She could be wrong about his intention toward her, but she doubted it. She smiled. He wanted riding lessons and that was exactly what he'd get. Tapping the icon to process the application, a series of programs went into effect, one sending an acceptance to Caleb Masters.

CHAPTER THREE

CAL'S TRUCK ROLLED to a stop near Piper's horse barn. He cut the engine and got out. Today was his first lesson. Although he didn't have the apprehension he felt when his mom let go of his hand on his first day of kindergarten, he felt something that he couldn't quite identify. After all, it wasn't like he was going to have to scope out the schoolyard and establish himself as friend or foe. He liked Piper and believed somewhere deep down she liked him, too.

Cal went into the barn. He hadn't visited his horses yet. There were twenty of them when he bought the ranch. The Christensens sold ten before he took possession. Seven others were contracted for, leaving three that Cal agreed to take. He found their stalls in the barn. As he stopped at each stall, they came to him, friendly, seeking something to eat probably. Cal had nothing. No fruit, no carrots, no sugar cubes. Still, they appeared interested in him.

He remembered their names from previous visits, yet they were printed on the outside of the half gate where they were stalled. Cal spent a few minutes with them before heading out to find Piper and mentally agreeing to come by and exercise the horses himself.

Outside, he spotted Piper carrying a saddle. Slinging it over the slated fence, she settled it next to one that was already there. His footsteps, crunching on the hard ground, must have alerted her to his nearness. She turned and looked at him. Her hair was under a hat and pulled back behind her ears. The sun made her skin glow golden and as usual her hair flamed as it flowed across her shoulders. Cal moved before he realized he was doing it. He felt as if she were drawing him to her. She had no smile, although her face was relaxed. Walking with purpose, he stopped short of stepping into her personal space.

"Good morning," Cal said.

Piper nodded, saying nothing.

"This is a different kind of saddle," he said, indicating the one she had set on the fence.

"It's a trick saddle." She reached out and touched it affectionately as if it meant something sentimental to her. Cal was used to a Western saddle and recognized the one on her left. The other one had marked differences, most notably the saddle horn was longer, straighter and with smaller nubs on top. Immediately, he recognized it would be easier to hold.

"I see," Cal said and shifted his glance away from the fence. "What made you change your mind?"

"I haven't changed my mind," she replied.

Cal raised his eyebrows in confusion.

"It depends on you," she said.

"How's that?" She gave him a long stare. Cal wondered if she was going to explain.

"First, I want to make sure you're serious."

"Why wouldn't I be serious? I signed up for daily lessons."

"That in itself is unusual."

"Most people don't jump in with both feet on the first day?" he asked.

She nodded. "In fact, I've never had a daily student."

Cal wanted to smile but forced his face to remain still.

"With my schedule, I can't take a daily student. I have full classes already."

"I understand," he said. "However, I am serious and I'll come as often as you can fit me in. I really want to learn. Why would you think anything different?"

"This is not my first time having someone give me a reason that isn't exactly true."

Cal was unsure of what she meant. But she'd figured him out. He wanted to know more about her and this was his way of doing it. Learning to do the tricks was a bonus. He wanted that, too, though.

"You said first, so what's your next reason?"

"There's only one more and that's up to you and your ability with a horse. I need to see if you're ready to start learning tricks."

"That's fair," he said. "Shall we begin?"

She nodded.

Cal moved to take the saddle from the fence, assuming he had to saddle his horse. Piper held up her hand, stepping in front of him to stop his movement.

"What are you doing?" she asked.

"I thought you wanted me to saddle a horse. I was going to carry it into the barn."

"Not yet," she said. "There's some basic information we need to go over first. Then I'll show you a few stunts before you even get near a horse. Got it?"

"Got it." He nodded.

She gave a shake of her head and Cal noticed that her glance quickly reached his face before turning away. Piper bent, stepped through the fence and stood up on the other side.

"You said you could ride. Let's see what you can do." She smiled, but again it quickly disappeared.

Cal joined her on the other side of the fence. As if on cue, a groomsman led two saddled horses into the paddock. Neither of them were Cal's horses. Piper took the reins of one and swung effortlessly into the saddle. Cal could see she did this with ease. He mounted the other horse, knowing she was watching him for any error. There was none. Cal had been riding since he was a teen, learning on his grandmother's farm in Connecticut. Horses were one of the pleasures he could count on no matter where in the world he worked. There were even times when travel by horse was the only way to reach remote areas.

His instinct was to take off at a full run, let her know that he was more than an adequate horseman. But he knew that she would reprimand him for not being careful with an unknown animal. So he walked the horse around the fenced yard, then, step by step, changed to a strut, to a canter and then to a ride. Going through the open gate, he headed for the ridge between their two properties. He didn't have to look back to know she was following him.

It felt good as he leaned forward, his head low to the wind. Hooves beat a steady rhythm beneath him. Cal felt the urge to go on and on. The ridge seemed to extend forever and he was ready to ride it all. Piper didn't call out to him. She caught up and they rode together. Cal glanced at her, smiling. Her face was slightly turned away from him, but he thought he saw a wispy upturn at the edge of her lips.

After several minutes they pulled up and slowed the horses to a walk. When they stopped, Cal slid to the ground, holding on to the reins. Piper did the same.

"Where did you learn to ride like that?" she asked as they gave the horses a rest.

"Often when I'm on a job site, there are no fitness centers around. The areas can be remote, sometimes mountainous, sometimes flat land. Equipment may need to be airlifted in the case of building roads where there are none. That's when a horse is the best mode of getting to a location. But mainly, I ride for pleasure and enjoy it."

"Self-taught?"

"Not exactly. I had lessons as a child. My brother and I used to have competitions, pretending we were at the Kentucky Derby and seeing who could get to the post fastest."

"I suppose you won?" she said dryly.

"He's the more athletic one. I made it there first a few times, but he holds the record."

"Well, it's paid off," she said.

"So, do you think I could learn to do the type of riding you do…in ten lessons?" he teased.

She laughed. It was the first time Cal had heard that. He liked it and wondered why she didn't laugh more often.

He watched her as she appeared to think about his request. Frowning at the sun, she used her hand to shade her eyes even with her hat on. She looked him straight in the eye.

"Are you sure? I know I've asked this before. Learning won't be easy."

"But it'll be fun," Cal said.

"It's harder than it looks. And it's dangerous. You could break a bone."

"I can do that anytime."

Cal figured she'd pulled back on the severity of injuries that could befall him. "I've already signed your waiver regarding the dangers of working with horses. And I'm a careful horseman."

Piper stared at the trail they had just covered. Had his wild ride been reckless? It wasn't. He and his brother had done worse things, but he was older and wiser now.

Her shoulders rose and fell in a resigned gesture. "You're on. Let's go back and we'll get you organized."

As they approached the fenced area, the corral now contained two horses, both ready with trick saddles.

One of the stable hands came to them as they dismounted and took the horses they'd ridden.

"So first, there are the saddles," Piper said as they stopped at the original ones still perched on the fence. "The saddle to learn tricks on is distinct from a riding saddle."

"Just as Western and English saddles are different," Cal supplied.

"Exactly."

She went through the differences he'd noted before their ride, confirming his thoughts on the saddle horn being easier to hold on to.

"Got it?" she asked.

"Most of it," he said. She didn't speak fast, but there was a lot that he needed to remember, even though his hands itched to mount the horse and get riding.

"Stay here," Piper commanded. She walked to one of the already-saddled horses and swung her lithe body into the leather seat. Cal thought of the first time he'd seen her in the distance, riding with her hair free to the wind. He was sure he'd always think of her that way—a free spirit, an uninhibited maverick.

He watched as she went through a series of tricks: standing on her hands, riding backward, dismounting while the horse was in motion, and running alongside it and then mounting the horse again when she and the animal were perfectly in sync. Cal thought of old black-and-white movies he and his brother used to watch on rainy Sundays. They were dated and simple, but an actor's ability to jump on a horse from impossible angles was always a plus in his eyes.

Piper slipped back into the saddle and stopped the horse in front of him. She jumped to the ground, grabbed a rope and attached it to the saddle horn.

"Your turn," she said, a glint in her eye.

Cal was winded just from watching her, yet there was no trace of breathlessness in her voice and not a single drop of sweat on her brow.

Piper connected a long leather strap to the bridle.

"What's that for?" he asked.

"So I can control the horse and keep you safe. Now, mount the horse."

Cal did as he was told. Holding both the rope and strap, she took him through several exercises with the horse remaining still. Eventually, they began to move, and with his first try of pushing himself off the saddle and pulling his legs up, he fell. Looking up at Piper from the dusty ground, he expected sympathy.

He got none.

Getting up, he glanced at her and, without a word, mounted the horse again. Trying the same routine, he achieved the same result— the ground. Yet Cal was not done. He tried the stunt over and over, but mainly the result was him looking up from the dust. Finally, he managed to stay on while holding his weight on his hands and extending one leg behind him. Thrilled with his accomplishment, he wanted to do it again. Piper let him do it three more times before she indicated it was enough for one day.

"I'm going to feel this in the morning," Cal said, taking a gingerly step forward as he rubbed his obviously sore backside.

"You will," she agreed.

He could almost hear the laughter in her voice.

"You know, if I was a betting man, I'd swear you had me do more than my share of falls."

"I wanted to make sure you learned this lesson before any of the others."

Cal rubbed his backside again. "I'd say you did that."

"That's all for today," Piper said. "I'll see you next week."

"Not tomorrow?" Cal raised his brows.

"Not tomorrow," she said.

He didn't want to wait a week to see her again. As they returned the horses to the barn, Cal said, "Then have dinner with me tonight."

Piper stiffened as if delivering bad news. "Sorry, I have plans."

Cal knew she'd refuse and he was prepared for it. He didn't give up easily and hoped she'd respect that. "You have to eat."

Her eyes narrowed. "Mr. Masters—"

"Cal," he corrected.

She looked at him. "Cal, you've been in this valley long enough to know that I make it a policy to not get involved."

"We'll be eating, sharing a table. It's not a date," Cal said. "It's just that I'm tired of eating alone. And I imagine you are, too. When I worked at a site, there was always someone to eat with. I'll be at the diner at six." He paused. Then speaking slowly, he said, "If you change your mind."

He tipped his hat and left her. Cal had come across some needy people in his life, but Piper seemed to need human contact more than most. He'd seen the signs before. He'd even been on the receiving end of that kind of misery. Whatever she was hiding was complex, emotional, and definitely involved a man.

BY SIX THIRTY Piper had not shown and Cal gave up on her coming at all. It was not like he had a solid confirmation from her. In fact, it was the exact opposite. Ordering a steak, baked potato and peas, he sat back to wait for his meal. He thought of pulling his phone out and sending a text to his brother but decided against it. He might tell him he was waiting for a woman who'd rebuffed him and nosy Jake Masters would surely call instead of replying by text.

Cal lifted his water glass and noticed the door open and Piper walking through it. She looked around, obviously searching for him. Cal drew in a surprised but relieved breath. He stood and smiled, waving her over. His heart lifted at seeing her. She was no longer dressed in riding gear but wore a blue short-sleeved shirt, tight blue jeans and black hand-tooled boots. A white sweater was slung over one arm.

"I'd given up on you," Cal said as she slipped into the booth across from him.

"I needed to talk to a friend at the hotel. Since I was already in town and hungry, I'm here."

"You know you put a lot of energy into pushing people away," he said.

Piper huffed at him. The reaction was expected. Leaning forward, he lowered his voice. "Why don't we put all that aside and share a good meal?"

Her nod was so slight, he barely saw it. The waitress came over at that moment.

"I've already ordered," he told Piper. He glanced at the waitress. She was tall, with soft curves and an abundant smile. She wore her blond hair pulled back in a long braid that dangled down her back. "Piper, this is Ally, short for Alicia. She owns the diner."

He knew Piper didn't mix with a lot of folks and he also knew that having friends in town was a plus no matter where you lived. Cal had been to the diner several times. He knew Ally had only owned the cute eatery for four years and she was from Nebraska.

So she wasn't original to the area. And Piper probably didn't know her.

Piper nodded.

"I heard you were in town a while ago. Glad to meet you," Ally said, her smile friendly.

Piper gave her a smile. "It's good to meet you, too."

Cal noticed Piper didn't say she was happy to meet her. He got the implication that while Piper's words were genuine, her position still said *back away*.

"I'll have the same thing he's having," she said.

Cal watched Ally tuck her order book in her apron and leave.

"You don't know what I ordered."

"I'm not picky," she said. "And I've had the food here before, usually takeout, but I trust it's good."

"You said you were visiting a friend. Was that the only reason you came?"

Her eyes dropped to the table before she looked straight at him. "I had another engagement."

So she wasn't eating and working alone, Cal thought, but did not bring it up. "And you canceled it to have dinner with me?" His smile widened before he noticed her shaking her head.

"My friend canceled. Something came up at work and she had to take care of it. So I was free."

Whatever the circumstances, she was here now and he was glad. Ally returned and set drinks in front of them, giving him a cover for the smile he knew was curving his mouth. Lifting his glass, he offered Piper a toast. "Her loss, my win." He drank. She did not. "I thought you were pretty much a loner here and didn't participate with the town much."

"I'm not a total recluse," she defended. "I know people here and Meghan has been a friend of mine since we were children."

"Meghan? From the hotel?"

Piper's eyes opened wider. Cal noted her surprise.

"We met a few days ago," he explained. "I was exploring the hotel, looking at the architecture from the early twentieth century, and she asked if she could be of assistance."

Piper showed the shadow of a smile again. "She's like that. A natural when it comes to customer service and making people feel comfortable."

Cal nodded. He came away with that impression.

"What did the two of you do as children?" he asked.

Piper shifted in her seat but seemed to relax a bit when she settled. "The usual things kids do, horseback riding, swimming, chasing after boys."

Cal was taken aback by her last comment. But Piper smiled and Cal wasn't disappointed. It was everything he thought it would be, bright, happy and full of joy, even better than the first time he saw it. For a split second, the sadness that was constantly with her seemed to abate.

Their food arrived and conversation was put on hold. Seemed they were both hungry.

"I know you're an engineer," Piper said after a couple of bites of her steak.

"I am. When I finished school, my plan was to work in the US, but I was offered a job in Argentina and the opportunity to keep traveling was appealing. I grew to love new places and new jobs. I stuck with it. I've worked in most countries, practically every continent."

"What do you engineer?"

"Mostly bridges and roads, but I have been involved in channeling water systems and working on high-rise buildings. Once, I even worked in a toy factory making carts for wooden horses with wheels that rotated and a Ferris wheel for a six-year-old girl that she could turn on and off by remote control."

"That sounds like fun. The look on the child's face when she saw it moving must have made all the work worth it."

Cal was surprised at her perception. He could still see the wide eyes of little Maia when he watched her push the remote's button and the lights came on, the music began and the wheels began to revolve.

"It was extremely rewarding," he whispered. Realizing he was talking to himself, he straightened and offered his attention to Piper.

"You like children?"

"Never been around them much, but I like them. They're so open and honest," Cal said.

"I suppose so."

"Does that mean you haven't been around kids, either?"

"Not many," she said.

Cal noticed she didn't elaborate. Her tone said her experience wasn't positive.

"They pay you with hugs," he said. He sat back. "The first time a kid hugged me, I wasn't expecting it. I found her crying. She and a friend had been playing, then a tug-of-war broke out and the doll was torn. I fixed it using some duct tape and fishing line. You'd have thought it was made of rubies. She threw her arms around my neck and gave me the tightest hug. Emotions I didn't know existed surfaced."

"So you want to have children of your own?"

"I do," he said. Cal hadn't really thought of it until that moment. Maybe it was the ranch, all that space and the huge house. A family should live there. Clearing his throat, he dislodged the images of that little girl and focused on Piper. "Well, that's me. What about you? Before you came back to the Valley to give riding lessons, what did you do?"

The look she gave him was baffling.

"What?" he asked.

"Nothing." She shook her head quickly as if dislodging a thought. "I worked in Hollywood."

"Actress?" She was certainly pretty enough to be on the screen. "I haven't seen many movies. Not a lot of free time, I'm afraid."

"I wasn't on the screen, at least not that anyone would know it was me," Piper said. "I worked as a stunt coordinator."

Cal stopped eating and stared at her. "That's why you have the gymnastics equipment and keep up with the stunt riding."

"Something like that," she concurred. "They're mainly for exercise, but I love riding."

There was more to it than that, Cal thought, but he didn't ask. There had to be a reason why a beautiful woman hid herself away on a ranch alone, except for caretakers and ranch hands. Cal could only wonder what had driven her to this point in her life.

"Hollywood sounds interesting. What does a stunt coordinator do?"

"Mainly I design stunts for the screen."

"That's a little simplistic," Cal said. "What do you mean by *design*?"

"I began as a stuntwoman but moved into coordination. And yes, there's a lot more to it. Mainly, I help with making up the sequences and putting together all the steps involved in capturing a stunt on film. Everything from the scaffolding to the lighting to the position of every camera. What you see on the screen..." She paused. "If you ever watched a screen, what you would see is due to the careful work of a large team of highly professional people."

He nodded to her, remembering that he didn't watch many movies or television programs.

Piper continued. "There are a lot of moving parts necessary to make a movie. Stunts are only a small section of the overall plan."

"And you love your part in bringing those stories to the screen," Cal stated. He could hear it in her voice. As much as she tried to keep her voice level, he could hear the undercurrents of hope, pride and love.

Piper held on to her thoughts by taking a bite of her food. "I did," she finally said.

"Did? You don't love it anymore?"

She looked up, above his head at the top of the windows, then back at him. "I thought we were just going to have dinner, not delve into personal history."

Cal nodded. Obviously, she did not want to discuss her past. "Conversation is part of getting to know each other, but I'll postpone any discussion until you decide you can trust me."

"Why would I want to trust you?"

For some reason, Cal thought she'd spoken before remembering to hold back her words.

Cal smiled. "I'm a trustworthy guy. I know you don't know me well, yet." He added *yet* to signal her that it was only a matter of time before that happened. "So far, you know I'm an engineer. Worked all over the world. I have one brother, who lives in New York. He was married last year."

"Why are you telling me all this?" Piper asked. "Is it merely conversation or do you think I'll do the same thing and reveal my family history?"

"Since you want to keep your secrets, I thought I'd tell you some of mine," he said.

"A job, family, these don't sound like secrets," she said. "Not unless there's some skeleton you're going to reveal."

"No skeletons. Although my brother is a doctor, and for a couple of years, he couldn't use his right arm."

Piper's eyes narrowed and her brows knitted together.

"A surgeon?" she asked.

"Trauma surgeon."

"Involved in a bombing in France?" She said it as if she knew more about it than her words conveyed.

"You know him?" Cal shouldn't be surprised. Dr. Jake Masters had an international reputation.

"I've never met him. One of the producers wanted to make a movie of his life. From what I hear, he's done some pretty miraculous things. But he refused to even discuss the subject."

"That would be Jake," Cal said. "He was an angry man for a long while. Then he met Lauren, his wife. She turned him around."

"Love will do that." Piper's voice was a whisper, but Cal heard it. He also heard the same undercurrent that told him something was wrong. Someone had wronged her romantically, and from her actions, she was never going to allow it to happen again.

DINNER WASN'T TOTALLY AWKWARD, Piper thought, though she was relieved that it was over. She left the restaurant more friendly with Cal than when she entered it. He didn't press her to talk about her past, even though he volunteered that he always liked finding out how things worked and that had led him to engineering. Silently, he walked her to her truck and stopped.

"I'll see you home," he told her.

"That won't be necessary," she protested.

"Yes, it is." He was adamant and she made no further argument.

The drive seemed to take longer than usual. Piper continually checked her rearview mirror for the lights of his truck. Cal was a safe distance behind her, and he didn't waver from keeping up with her speed. She reconsidered why he'd wanted her to eat with him. He was new to the Valley and she was his closest neighbor, but she thought there was more to it. Maybe it was attraction, yet during his lesson, he didn't make any personal or romantic type of overtures. They'd both understood Montana was a temporary stop on their life path. Was that the reason?

Did like souls want to gather together? Were they like souls? And was he romantically interested in her? Piper knew there was an interest. Yet neither of them planned to remain in Waymon Valley for long. For him, that leaving might come sooner than her chance to return to Hollywood, if she ever could.

Hadn't Cal said he'd traveled around the world? And she wanted to get back to making movies. She loved what she did.

She pulled into her driveway and got out of the truck just as Cal got out of his.

"I'm all right." She waved, hoping he would get back inside.

He didn't.

She noticed how he walked as he approached her. The lights of his truck were still on and it silhouetted him. He had strong legs, great for horseback riding, and a determined stride. His arms hung loose and relaxed.

"I never noticed how dark and quiet it was out here at night," he said, facing her.

Piper looked up at the starry sky. "It's beautiful."

"It is," he sighed.

"And peaceful." Piper spread her hands. "Can't you hear the cicadas and crickets?"

He cocked his head as if he'd just noticed them. "With this vastness, they seem dwarfed. Isn't it a little scary being here alone?"

"I'm not alone. I have ranch hands and a caretaker, a housekeeper."

"Do any of them stay after the sun sets?"

She took a moment before shaking her head. "But I'm perfectly safe."

"You're alone, several miles from a road and even further from the town."

"I can take care of myself." She tried to keep the anger from her voice, but she'd heard this argument before. "I have an alarm system and the caretaker has several dogs that roam the property."

"That's still not enough protection. Break-ins can happen anywhere."

"And you think I'm vulnerable?"

He nodded.

To prove her point, as Piper knew she'd have to, she quickly hooked her foot around one of his legs and pulled him off balance. She was smaller and weighed less than he did, but she had the element of surprise on her side, not to mention years of practice. He went down like a brick wall when all the mortar had eroded and a soft wind would topple it.

Standing above him with her hands on her hips, she said, "See?"

In answer, Cal scissored his legs, catching hers and bringing her down to the ground with him. Quickly, he pinned her under him.

"Yes, I see," he said, as if he had the upper hand.

Piper had been in this position before. Then it was a stunt, but it didn't matter now. She knew what she had to do.

"Let me go and I promise I won't hurt you," she said.

Cal laughed. It was the response she expected.

He wasn't holding on to her hands. Bad idea. Piper did two things simultaneously. She raised her knee, making no contact, just as she'd do in a movie. Since Cal expected contact, he braced and shifted. Using the time she had, she tossed him aside, the dust and dirt pluming as he landed hard.

Piper scrambled several yards away.

Cal lay on the ground, likely stunned and with the wind knocked out of him. For a few seconds she was worried. She'd only ever performed this as a stunt.

A moment later he lifted his head and

rolled over, sitting up to face her. "I give," he said, raising a hand as if she was about to launch another attack. "You can take care of yourself. I'll never question you again."

Piper relaxed, moving into a standing position. Offering him her hand, she gladly pulled him up.

"Who taught you those moves?" Cal asked.

"Hollywood," she answered.

Cal frowned.

"So, what are you doing here? You said you were a stunt coordinator. No filming happening in this county, is there?"

"Technically, I'm retired," she said.

"Aren't you a little young for retirement? Were you injured and had to stop?"

He looked her over as if he'd find scars from her mishaps.

"The truth is I defied the odds," Piper said. "I've never been hurt. Not even a scratch that needed cleaning." Raising her arms, she showed off her flawlessness.

"I'm one of the lucky ones," she told him. "Stunts are designed with every possible outcome examined. Safety first." She echoed the mantra of her profession but did not answer his question about being retired.

She had her reasons and at this point she wasn't ready to share.

Piper dropped her chin and looked away so Cal couldn't see the tenseness in her features. The truth was she didn't feel lucky. She'd always prided herself on doing exactly what was required for a stunt with unblemished precision. But doubt had seeped into her mind and taken hold. She'd done something wrong and she couldn't deny it.

Stepping up on the bottom rung of the porch stairs, she found Cal was still a little startled by her actions.

"Think I'm all right here alone?"

"You're a wonder," he said, holding his hands up in surrender. "Maybe you can protect me instead."

"It's possible," she conceded. "Thank you for dinner, Cal." Her voice reminiscent of a formal teacher. It was a voice she used for students. "I enjoyed myself and our conversation."

"I did, too. I hope we can do it again."

It was on the tip of her tongue to refuse.

"You have to admit that sharing a meal is better than eating alone," he encouraged.

Piper didn't speak for a moment. "I'm busy and I prefer to make my own meals."

"Maybe you could cook for me and I can do the same for you," he suggested humorously.

"Naomi cooks for you," she told him.

"Not every night," Cal defended.

"Can you cook?" Piper's brows rose.

"I can," he said confidently. "I'm good at some meals. Not a gourmet, but I have skills, a couple of favorites."

The porch light showed anticipation in his eyes. Was he hoping she would go for it? Piper considered it, weighing his comment for some time. She asked herself if he was telling the truth or just throwing an invite out there like a hook trying to land a fish.

Finally, she replied, "Like I said, I prefer my own cooking."

CHAPTER FOUR

THE HOTEL EMILY sat near the train station in Waymon Valley. It had more than one dining room after renovations Meghan had spearheaded a few years ago. The dining room they went in was the original one. It still held some of the features and all of its original charm. The coffered ceiling with its dark beams had been fashioned and installed by Meghan's great-great-great-grandfather Luke Evans.

Piper had attended many events in this building. From cotillions to weddings to the Hunter's Ball and family dinners. Sitting in the center of the formal gold-and-white room, she waited for Meghan to get a break in her duties and join her for their postponed lunch.

Piper gave the menu more attention than it deserved. She didn't want to look around, didn't want to know if the stares and whispers she was subject to were happening. When she used to visit her aunt and uncle while working in Hollywood, her friends and the community were awed by her. Now, with her, they seemed wary and disappointed.

"Small-town girl makes good" hits the local papers and is quickly tossed on the recycle pile. But "Small-town girl accused of doing bad" is discussed ad nauseam.

Cal had heard the rumors. When he first got to town and people knew his ranch was next to Piper's, they volunteered tidbits. Cal still wanted to be friends with her. She smiled at that. Their time in the diner and their dinner conversation came back to her. The after-dinner events were also pressed into her memory, just as Cal's body had been when he had her underneath him on the ground. Her face grew warm at the thought.

Before she had time to revisit the rest of the night, Meghan slid into the chair opposite Piper. A waiter immediately appeared and took their order. Piper knew it was because everyone who worked at the Emily essentially reported to Meghan. It was a happy workplace and Meghan was a fair employer. The problem was it kept Meghan so busy, she had no social life. What a pair the two of them were, Piper thought. Meghan wanted a relationship and Piper didn't.

"Before I forget," Meghan began, a little out of breath. "I'm having some friends over next Friday. I expect you to come."

"Meghan, no."

Meghan was shaking her head, cutting off any excuse Piper might voice.

"It's time." She paused. "Besides, most of the guests are people you've known for years."

"They'll want to ask about the accident."

"They won't ask," Meghan assured her.

"But I'll see the question in their faces."

"I can't prevent what you presume is in someone's face," Meghan smirked. "Eight o'clock. Don't be late."

Piper gave her a long look. In the back of her mind, she knew Meghan had a point. It had been a year since she returned to the Valley and the only people she communicated with were the cashier in the grocery store and several of her students' parents. She'd refused all invitations, except Cal's offer to join him for dinner, and she almost hadn't gone to that one.

The waiter arrived with their food. Piper felt he took an unusual amount of time as he elegantly set things on the table. She watched his movements but really saw nothing. Her mind was someplace else.

"Piper?" Meghan's voice called her back from her daydreaming.

She looked up.

"You're not listening to me."

"I'm sorry. What did you say?"

"I said, don't keep me in suspense," Meghan repeated when the waiter departed. "I've been waiting to find out how your date with Cal went."

"It wasn't really a date. We ate at the diner." Piper glanced at the opulent surroundings and couldn't help comparing them to the simple decor of the diner.

"It was a date," Meghan stated adamantly. "So how was it?"

"Fine."

"Fine," Meghan imitated.

"What do you want me to say? We met. We ate. I went home."

"That sucks," Meghan said.

Piper gave her a warning look.

"I have a busy hotel to run," Meghan reminded her. "Am I going to have to wait until the next century or are you going to just tell me?"

Piper's shoulders dropped. She knew she had to tell Meghan or they would go round and round until Meghan got the story out of her.

"It was pleasant."

"Pleasant? That's what you say about someone you don't like."

"I never said I liked him."

Meghan rolled her eyes. "What did you two talk about?"

Piper had enjoyed dinner. It had been a long time since she spent any time with a man. Cal was interesting, but she pushed thoughts of him aside. She wasn't ready for another relationship. She'd been betrayed by more than one man in her life, and this wasn't the time to open her heart to someone new.

"Piper," Meghan warned.

"Sorry," Piper said. "We talked about normal things, his job, his travels. Did you know his brother is Dr. Jake Masters?"

"The surgeon? Wasn't he hurt a few years ago?"

Piper nodded. "He's recovered, married and, according to Cal, doing well."

"That's good to hear. But back to dinner. Did you enjoy talking to him?"

"I did." Piper smiled. "He's easy to talk to."

Meghan leaned forward as if Piper had just revealed a juicy piece of gossip. "Much different than the Hollywood scene?"

Piper laughed. "Not much. Most of those people are real to each other. It's only the screen personas and the marketing machines that make the public think differently about them. But Cal—" She broke off.

"Go on," Meghan prompted. "But Cal what?"

"He's different from all of them."

"How do you feel about him?"

"Feel?" Her brows rose. "I barely know him."

"True, but we both know that when there is an attraction between two people, it deserves to be explored. Do you like him enough to want to go out with him again?"

Piper turned over Meghan's question, coming up with several answers and discarding them. She'd told Cal she didn't want to repeat their dinner. Not in those words, but the implication was there. She knew it wasn't the truth when she told him that. There were too many things flowing through her mind. Xavier was one of them. Being hurt again. Getting involved with someone who wasn't planning to stick around. Her own issues regarding her future or lack of a future.

Meghan waited patiently for her answer. Did she want to go out with Cal again? It didn't take long for Piper to answer the question in her mind. It took a while for her to voice the words.

"I wouldn't mind," she whispered.

"Did he ask you?"

She nodded.

"What did you say?" Meghan's excitement jumped up a notch.

"I told him I enjoyed my own cooking."

Meghan's face fell. "Are you planning on living alone forever? I know Xavier hurt you, but you can't judge all men by him."

"I'm not judging. I'm just not ready," Piper said.

"It's been a year, Piper. When are you going to be ready?"

"I don't know."

Meghan gave up on her then. "Well, did he take you home?"

"I had my own truck. He walked me to the parking lot and followed me all the way to my door. Not that I needed that."

"But he's a gentleman," Meghan finished.

Piper admitted that to herself. "Apparently, he was reared to be respectful of women."

"So, no kiss good-night?"

THIS WAS ALL Meghan's fault, Piper thought as she stood at the fence watching her horses exercise. Why had she asked that question? Piper hadn't thought about kissing Cal. Now it was all she could think of. As soon as Meghan mentioned a good-night kiss, it suddenly dropped on her how disappointed she was that he hadn't tried.

She expected him to arrive for his lesson in a few minutes. Piper had told him daily lessons didn't fit her schedule. But when Cal called earlier, asking if she'd had a cancellation, she worked him in. Piper blamed Meghan for this change of tack, too. Why didn't she stick to her rule? The truth was, she had the time. But he got under her skin. She wanted to see him, she admitted, talk to him even though she knew he was as dangerous as a hot branding iron. Piper needed to be on her guard, get her emotions under control. Neither of them was looking for a relationship. She knew beginning one would mess up both their lives and she wasn't entertaining another messy future.

Bringing her attention back to the ranch, Piper shook her head as if she could shake off the troublesome thoughts that were forefront in her mind. The horses helped. She could pinpoint the exact moment when she fell in love with horses. As a child, she'd seen them in books, but it was her first time at the ranch that she saw a live horse and her love for the animal began. Her aunt told her that her eyes grew as large as the horse. Nothing had attracted her that way since. She'd spent every waking moment learning about them and learning to ride. While Cal had trained on his side of the world, she'd done the same on hers.

Horses were the reason she got her first stunt job. Standing against the fence now, she had the same rush of feeling as she watched the horses go about their playful exercises as she'd had her first day on set with cameras rolling.

Her phone rang. Pulling it from her back pocket, she expected it to be Cal canceling his lesson. But she was surprised to see Tamara St. John's name and image appear on her small screen.

"Tamara," Piper said, happy to hear from her.

Tamara should have been on screen as a sexy ingenue instead of a stuntperson. She was outgoing, talented, and had a killer smile. She even had the perfect name for the silver screen. Piper could see it as a credit: *starring Tamara St. John*. Yet Tamara chose to pursue stunt work instead of acting.

Piper had hired her for Xavier's last project and Tamara had proved herself. Not only was she a master at movement and makeup, but she was nearly a magician in her ability to become someone else. And even though Piper had left the industry behind, she still considered Tamara her friend. So when calls appeared on her phone from Tamara, Piper always answered.

"How's it going?" Piper asked after their greeting.

"Fine. Busy. We just wrapped a job."

She heard the words, but she also heard the hesitation in her friend's voice. The two had always been able to read each other's feelings. Often, they could share a joke just by looking at each other. "What is it?"

Tamara sucked in a long breath. "Like you, I've decided to make a change and I need your help."

"Sure. What can I do?"

"I want you to come back," Tamara said.

Piper's back went up immediately. She stood up straighter. "Tamara—"

"Let me finish," Tamara interrupted.

"Okay."

"No one knows this yet, so you have to keep it a secret."

Piper had no idea where this was going. She waited for Tamara to continue.

"I'm thinking of starting my own stunt business."

"Tamara, that's wonderful," Piper said excitedly. She was also relieved that something more tragic hadn't happened.

Piper was thrilled for her friend. She knew Tamara would be successful. She was intelligent, well-liked by everyone and had a lot of connections.

"I want you to be my partner."

"No." Piper shook her head as if the two could see each other.

"Hear me out," Tamara said, her voice a little tight.

"There's nothing you can say that will get me back to California. I've been in that fire and it burns long and hot. Besides, I'd be a liability to your business. Xavier has seen to that."

"You know I don't believe Xavier. He's out for himself and no one else."

How well Piper agreed with that. It was too bad she hadn't known it when she was in a relationship with him.

"Things haven't been going that well for him since you left."

"You just said you finished a project."

"We did, but we don't have any new contracts, nothing big at least."

"He's not doing well?" Piper was unsure how she felt about that. She'd worked side by side with him for three years. The two had been more than friends, but he'd been the cause of her downfall. At least he'd assured it happened.

"He's still solvent and is holding on to

a few contracts for upcoming movies, but more and more jobs are going elsewhere. His plans seem more like do-overs than innovations. You were the brains behind him, and with you gone…" She left the sentence hanging.

Piper knew she'd given Xavier ideas to make the stunts better. Most, if not all, of his plans were eventually replaced with suggestions that came from her. Of course, he took credit for them. Piper assumed he'd share the limelight, but time and again he'd explain that she wasn't ready to design and handle a project alone. After a while, she'd let the argument go, reminding herself that Xavier owned the business and she voluntarily offered suggestions that he used. Piper also thought their relationship was more important.

Then he gave her the chance to design and create her own stunt project—one that would bear her name. She didn't realize it would turn out so badly and would forever be tattooed to her memory.

"Piper?" Tamara called. "Are you still there?"

"Sure, I'm here," she said, coming back from her checked past.

"Well, will you think about it?"

"I don't know, Tamara. Hollywood isn't very welcoming to someone who's been blamed for the crash-and-burn stunt I orchestrated."

"You have more friends here than you think. And I don't believe for a moment that the stunt wasn't designed perfectly. Something else happened."

Piper thought that, too. "Maybe," she said. "But there's no proof of that."

In fact, looking for that *something* was why she'd been going over and over the accident in her mind for the past twelve months. Something else had to have happened. But what? And why couldn't she find it?

"So, what do you think?" Tamara asked.

She frowned, thankful they weren't on a video call and that Tamara couldn't see the frown on her face. "Are you sure this is what you want to do? I thought you might want to go in front of the camera someday."

"I thought about that, but it's not for me. I like doing what I'm doing. It feels right, you know?"

She did know. Although the accident had divided her true friends from those who were loyal to Xavier, there were some good colleagues she still had on her side.

"Let me think about it," Piper said, knowing however long Tamara gave her to decide, her answer would have to be no. Owning her own stunt business was something Piper had thought of herself. Except Piper had never gone beyond the notion of striking out on her own.

"All right," Tamara said. "I'm willing to meet with you and discuss the details, show you my plan."

"That won't be necessary. I'll let you know."

"I'll give you a call next week," Tamara said.

Piper clicked the phone off and slipped it in her back pocket. With her hands on the fence, she hung her head thinking about Tamara's offer. It was exactly what she wanted. She'd dreamed of having her own company. She had the skills. She knew how to run a business. She was running the training school, although she only had three employees. She'd run Xavier's company almost single-handedly, organizing some of his financial processes and streamlining the crews that worked at various sites, in addition to designing and working out stunts.

Piper didn't know how long she stood there contemplating the phone call. She really wanted to go into business with her friend. Tamara had offered her the ability to do it, but Piper understood, probably better than her colleague, that if her name was associated with a stunt company, it was likely to fail. Who would trust her? A man had nearly died and the finger was pointed at her as the culprit. She couldn't allow Tamara to start a business that had her name attached to it. It would be doomed before it began.

"Lose your best friend?"

Piper jerked around as she heard Cal's voice. She'd been so absorbed in her thoughts that she hadn't detected either his truck or his footsteps. His presence surprised her. She was used to seeing him, but her heart raced every time he appeared. Today her heart hammered in her chest. Immediately, she thought of Meghan's teasing comment. No good-night kiss.

"No," she said automatically. "I was just thinking about all the things I have to do." That sounded hollow. She couldn't think why so many people said it when it was an obvious lie. She was sure Cal knew that, too.

"Then I feel guilty for pulling you away from your plans."

"I'll figure it all out," she said. "Ready for your lesson?"

He nodded.

Piper was relieved. Thoughts of Tamara and her offer flew out of her mind. The man before her left no room for thoughts of anything or anyone else.

"Come with me," she said. They started to head toward the barn with the gymnastics equipment. "I want to test your upper body strength."

"That sounds interesting," he said, reading something more into the statement than was intended. It hit the mark, forcing heat to flood Piper's face.

She pulled herself together as they moved from the bright outdoors to the subdued lighting of the gym.

"How do we do this?" Cal asked. "While I learned to ride a horse, I've never really done gymnastics. I was more a basketball and soccer kind of guy."

"Basketball is good conditioning. Soccer is all lower body." She began to explain what she wanted him to do. "We start with the lower parallel bar." Putting her hand on it, she indicated the one he would begin with. "I want to know if you can support your body weight with your arms."

"Didn't I already do that the other night, or are you thinking I was supporting myself on a different part of my anatomy?"

She flashed a look at him. Even without a smile on his face, he was teasing her.

"I don't want a repeat of that battle," she said, remembering their skirmish on the ground in front of her house.

He shrugged. Piper wondered if he thought she was challenging him. She wasn't. She was too busy trying to keep her mind on the lesson. He didn't make it easy. He was close to her and he made her nervous. She didn't know why. Not even Xavier had made her feel like this when she was initially attracted to him.

"This is the only one we'll be using. I'll show you what I want you to do." She grabbed the bar with both hands, bent her knees and slowly jumped up until her thighs were on the bar. Spreading her hands away from her body, she was completely balanced on the bar.

"That doesn't look like it'll help my upper body strength," Cal said. "Not that I haven't done this before."

Another past scene skated through her mind. Cal had tested the parallel bars after they reassembled them on the day they met. How had she forgotten that? Still, this exercise was necessary.

"It's to do with balance," she said. "You need to be able to balance yourself. On the horse, it will be a lot harder."

"I can attest to that," he joked.

Piper ignored him. At least she tried. Placing her hands back on the bar, she swung herself away from it and raised her legs several inches off the floor using the bar to hold herself up.

Jumping down, she moved aside but stayed close enough to spot him. Cal did as she had done. When it came to pushing himself away, he had trouble.

"Hollow your body," she said. "And push

your shoulders up and down." She gestured toward his stomach. When he didn't do it, she reached out and touched him, gently pushing in. Cal dropped to the floor.

"Excuse me," he said. "I'm ticklish."

Piper knew that wasn't true. She felt the jolt of awareness that passed between them. She'd coached enough people to know when her touch produced laughter. When she put her hand on Cal, it was something else entirely. She knew because every nerve ending she had was tingling. She would not touch him again. His body was warm and she didn't want her hands to convey her feelings.

"Try it again," she said.

He did it nearly perfectly. "Keep your legs straight," she said.

After several repetitions, he got it. "Great. You can get down now."

He jumped to the ground.

"What's the verdict?"

"You passed," she said. She knew the answer before she even checked. Piper had felt the strength of his core, and viewing the hard muscles of his arms, she had no doubt that he had enough strength for her planned lesson.

Leaving the gym, they walked back to the waiting horses. Piper demonstrated and Cal repeated her routine while she held on to a long tether. She had him get to his knees on the horse and extend one leg behind him as he'd done at the last lesson. He fell several times, but to his credit, he climbed back on and tried it again and again until he got it. Then he insisted on doing it several more times to make sure he had it. She liked that about him. The tumble to the ground didn't put him off, nor did he complain about hitting the hard earth. Since starting lessons, he had to be tender in more than one spot.

Meghan's question about a kiss came back to her and wouldn't leave. How long could she hold these feelings inside?

The hour passed quickly but stressfully. "That's it for today," Piper said, feeling relieved that she had finished without a personal mishap. Cal was doing very well, picking up the technique faster than anyone else she'd ever trained.

And that was the problem. At least it was one problem. She wanted to teach him more, encourage him to use his talent, but she couldn't. This was a hobby for him.

He wasn't planning to make a career of it. And she knew he came for lessons because he was attracted to her. Piper had to admit that despite her best efforts, Cal had found a way around her normal defenses. Thank goodness he didn't know it. Yet Meghan had guessed.

She should have refused to give him lessons. She could have said she only trained young kids, that she wasn't qualified to teach adults, that trick riding wasn't something she wanted to do. There were many excuses she could have come up with.

But she hadn't.

CAL RUBBED THE seat of his pants as they walked away from the horses. It had been a good workout and he was thankful that his first lesson was based on how to fall, since he'd had many spills. During his lessons as a boy, he rarely fell. When he worked on engineering sites, he was accomplished enough for travel by horse.

Piper's lessons were something else. With only two under his belt, he knew it was a different world, yet he was excited about it. And about being around her. She was clever, sure of herself and independent. That last could be a flaw. She was so independent that she didn't let anyone in, and if someone tried to get close, she pushed them away. She was so good at it that it had become second nature.

Cal had seen his brother go through the same phase after his accident. It was only his future wife, Lauren, who had the love, patience and fortitude to see past his anger and encourage him as he worked out his issues.

Cal couldn't help laughing at the stories he remembered Jake relating about how Lauren managed to get his mind off his problems. Cal wondered if that would work with Piper. He discarded the thought as soon as it came. No way could he pull off the zany moves like his sister-in-law had.

"What's so funny?" Piper asked.

Cal couldn't keep the smile off his face. "I was just thinking about my sister-in-law."

"I take it she's a character," Piper said.

"A wonderful one. I hired her to take care of my brother after his accident. He didn't know she was a doctor and she had an…" He paused, picturing the strong woman he loved like a sister dressed as a cartoon princess. "Let's just say she had an unorthodox method of dealing with my brother."

"One day you'll have to tell me the whole story."

"I will," Cal said. "You seem to be feeling better." They were approaching the house.

Piper looked at him questioningly. "What do you mean?"

"When I came up—" he glanced back at the fence where she'd been standing when he arrived "—you looked lost. You covered it quickly. I think that's the performer in you, but I saw it."

She looked away and didn't speak until they reached the steps leading to her house. "Would you like an iced tea?"

He nodded. "It would hit the spot."

While she went inside, Cal took a seat in one of the porch chairs. He wondered if she would tell him her story. It was obvious to him that she needed someone to talk to, and since he was still mostly a stranger, he might be the best person to hear her out.

The screen door opened and she backed out with a tray. Quickly, Cal got up and took it. He set it on the small table between the two chairs. Piper handed him one of the tall glasses and they took seats.

"Thank you," Cal said, sipping the sweet tea. "Perfect." It was exactly the way he liked it.

Cal remained quiet. He wanted her to take the lead.

"Why did you become an engineer?" Piper asked.

It wasn't the question he was expecting. "I was always interested in building things. I'd watch construction sites and tried to imagine how everything fit together. My grandmother saw the potential in me and enrolled me in a young engineers program when I was eight. I never looked back after that."

"And you've traveled a lot."

It was a statement, but Cal responded. "Yes, ma'am. Racked up a ton of frequent flyer miles."

She smiled as he hoped she would.

"What about you? Are you planning to do this for the rest of your life?" Cal extended his arm to gesture at the barn and stables.

Piper sat forward in her chair. "I once thought of owning my own stunt company."

"Once?" Cal questioned.

"It's over now. There's no way anyone would trust me."

He'd heard a rumor but didn't know the whole story. And Cal preferred to hear these sorts of things directly from the people involved, not second- or thirdhand. Piper's retreat to this ranch told him, even if rumor hadn't, that the problem had taken place in Hollywood and no one living here had been there.

"That phone call I had just before you came up…" she began.

He hadn't thought about it, but now he remembered her sliding her phone in her pocket.

"It was from a friend I used to work with in California. She's thinking of starting her own company and asked me to partner with her."

Cal smiled widely. "That's wonderful. It's a stunt company, right?"

"Right."

"Then why aren't you packing? It's what you want." Cal was excited for her, but he felt she was at odds. "Is this partner someone you don't want to go into business with?"

"It's not that. We're really good friends, and in another world, I'd be jumping for joy."

"But in this world?" he prompted.

"In this world, I'm a pariah."

"I don't understand," Cal said.

Piper laughed a little. "I'm sure you've heard the stories about me."

"Some of them. I don't usually listen to gossip. I'd rather hear the truth."

"Well, the truth, Mr. Masters, is that I was in charge of a stunt for an action movie. A man was nearly killed, and it was my fault."

Cal was stunned. He'd heard something to that effect, but he hadn't expected her to admit it so bluntly. He'd only known her a short while, but he'd seen, firsthand, the care she took to keep all her students safe. Accidents happened all the time. There was nothing that could be done about that. He thought about the gym equipment and how she could have been hurt because it wasn't secured correctly. A small tickle of doubt crept into his mind. Then he remembered she hadn't set it up.

"I've looked at the video of that stunt a hundred times and I don't see where anything should have gone wrong." She paused.

"But it did. And if I put my name anywhere near Tamara's, that's my friend who's starting the business, it'll never get off the ground."

"What does this stunt look like?" Cal asked. "Could I see the video?" He hadn't seen a lot of action movies or movies in general. Yet he would put his experience to use here. Now he wished he'd paid closer attention.

Piper hesitated. Again, Cal was surprised by her reaction. "It's all right if you don't want to. I was going to look at it from an engineering perspective."

"That might be good," she said. "It's just that no one else has offered any form of help since it happened. The suggestion took me by surprise."

"I'd like to help," Cal said, not really understanding what he expected to find. Yet her willingness to share touched something within him and he wanted to help. He wanted to erase that sad look from her eyes. Even when she smiled, the sadness was there, as if it had been chiseled into her.

She stood up, gently taking his arm and pulling him along. "Come with me."

CHAPTER FIVE

Piper led Cal to the small office off the kitchen. The laptop was already on and the video had been cued. She watched it several times a day hoping to see something different. She never did. Yet she continued to view it as if something about it would jump out and say, *Look, there. I'm not the cause.*

Taking a seat, Piper clicked the button to start the video. Cal leaned over her shoulder and suddenly she wished she'd moved the laptop to the large country kitchen. She felt his breath on her neck and stifled a shudder. There was a window that looked out in the direction of Cal's ranch house. She could see it as she worked at her desk. What would she think from now on? She'd be preoccupied with how she felt in this moment. His presence, his kindness unforgettable.

"Play that again," Cal said, pointing toward the screen. His voice jarred her. She almost jumped at the tremor so near to her ear. While he wasn't touching her, his nearness disconcerted her.

Piper pushed the slider back and restarted a section of the video. Cal concentrated on the screen. She tried also. She saw nothing out of the ordinary, nothing she hadn't seen a hundred times before.

"Do you see anything?" she asked.

"Nothing concrete, but if you don't mind, I'd like a copy of that."

"Sure," Piper said. She glanced over her shoulder. "Why?"

"I want to give it a closer look."

"Are you expecting to find something?" She wanted to know what he thought. Cal was another pair of eyes. She hadn't had that in the time she'd been looking at the stunt. If he saw something, she wanted to know what.

"I've never viewed a stunt this way before. When I do see a movie, I'm more involved in the action than looking at all the details. They would distract me when something wasn't quite true. So, I want to analyze this, see what it tells me."

"I can help. I know everything about it," she said.

"I'm sure you do. That might be the reason you don't see something."

"The forest for the trees?" she offered.

He nodded. "But there may also be nothing to see. You might have needed to be on the inside, seeing the stunt from the viewpoint of the person running." He indicated Austin Symmons, a veteran stuntman. "Or it just might have been an accident. But I'll look at it some more and tell you what I think."

Piper was grateful. She pulled up her email program and attached the video. Looking up at Cal, she asked for his address. He reached over her and typed it in. His arms were around her, effectively trapping her in her chair. Piper didn't want to pull away. She felt safe, cocooned, and she wanted that warmth to continue. She didn't know the name of the cologne Cal wore, but it had a mesmerizing effect on her. It reminded her of him: rugged, outdoorsy and laced with a hidden strength.

If he took to analyzing the video the way he took to learning how to ride a trick horse, maybe there was another explanation for what had happened.

She hoped so.

Cal pulled his arms back, sliding them across her shoulders. Fire burned over the places his fingers touched, then raced through her like water on a live wire. Piper swallowed hard, feeling both relieved and sorry that she couldn't hold on to him a little longer.

THE NIGHT WENT by slowly. Piper couldn't sleep. She kept thinking of Cal. Their time together, particularly his touches, which replayed over and over in her mind. She couldn't shake the memory of his arms around her. How special she felt, how she'd never felt that way before.

Piper wondered if he was able to sleep. Did he find anything in the video that she had missed? Frustration overtook her. She hadn't seen anything in the video to indicate what had caused the collapse that sent Austin into free fall.

Despite it still being dark, she pushed the covers aside and stood up. Muddling around the house until sunrise, she got dressed and clamped her hat on over her dark red locks. She marched out to the barn, where she saddled her favorite horse, Silver, and set out to exercise her, but found herself heading straight for Cal's ranch.

"I didn't see this coming," Naomi said when she swung the farmhouse door inward and found Piper standing on the porch.

"Good morning," Piper said, feeling a little out of place. She hadn't thought this through. She'd reacted. It was unlike her. She blamed it on wanting to know what Cal found, if anything. She refused to think any further about the reasons that had kept her tossing and turning all night.

"Come on in." Naomi smiled and pushed the screen door open. Standing back, she allowed Piper to enter. The moment Piper crossed the threshold, Naomi pulled her into her arms. The gesture had her remembering her years of running in and out of Naomi's kitchen.

She felt awkward. When she'd jumped down from Silver, she knew what she wanted to ask Cal, but now, confronted with the reality of the moment, she was at a loss for words. It wasn't like her. She'd fully acclimated to Hollywood life. Nothing surprised her and nothing threw her off. Yet she felt like an awkward fifteen-year-old coming home after running away and finding a distressed parent waiting for her.

"It's been a long time since you were in my kitchen," Naomi said. "You had anything to eat?"

Piper thought about that. It was always Naomi's first question when she appeared at the door. The truth was Piper hadn't even made coffee this morning. Usually, it was the first thing she thought of when her feet hit the bedside rug. But today her nerves were fueling her. Unable to speak, she shook her head.

"I see," Naomi said knowingly. "He's in the office." Jerking her head, she indicated the direction. "I'm sure you know where it is. It hasn't moved since the Christensens left."

Piper walked when she wanted to run toward the downstairs office. The Christensens had chosen to put the office one floor below all the typical noise of a large family.

Cal had his back to the large window and faced the door. He was concentrating on a huge computer screen but looked up when she filled the entrance. Her heart tripped when she saw him. While he looked perfectly groomed, he had the air of someone who'd been at it for hours. Piper's heartbeat raced. She had to stop doing this, she told herself. She knew she was going to see him. It wasn't like she'd come upon him by surprise and her heart raced as a result. Taking a long breath, she tried to calm herself.

Standing, he smiled, one of those happy-to-see-you smiles. And that caused another heart flutter.

"Good morning," he said, coming around the desk. "I guess you're an early riser, too."

"Not usually. We film sometimes in the early morning and sometimes in the middle of the night. Then there are days we go from one to the other. I'm sorry if I'm intruding. I hoped you'd be up."

"I've been up for a couple of hours," he said, drawing her farther into the room. "Come see what I've been doing."

He reached out as if to encircle her. Piper moved forward. Cal welcomed her. She didn't have to ask him for the details of his findings. He was inviting her to see for herself.

Cal pulled a second chair behind his desk.

She sat on his left and he brought up an image that looked like a schematic break-down of her stunt.

"What's this?" she asked, her voice showing a little surprise and awe at his detailed work.

"I have a program that I use when working on a design. It tells me a lot of things, one being dimensions, and an important amount of information on stress points, places where the metal can fail or if there's a weak connection."

"Do you see any of that in this?"

He shook his head. Piper smiled, happy that he hadn't, but sorry that nothing new had been found.

Cal frowned. "I don't have enough information to work with."

"What else do you need?"

"The weight of each of these girders, the type of screws used, the height from the ground, the wind speed and direction on that day."

"I'll get it," Piper said. "You need everything about everything, including the weight and height of the stuntman and possibly the sweat from my brow."

Cal laughed. "We can probably forgo that."

Piper laughed, too, and felt some relief afterward. She knew how uptight she felt and needed the relief.

"Do you have that information?" Cal asked.

"Most of it. The rest I can call Tamara and she'll send it to me."

"Tamara," he repeated. "The woman who wants you to start a company with her?"

"Good memory." Piper nodded.

"The information would fill in a lot of the holes. I like as few assumptions as possible."

"What are you going to do once you get it?" she asked.

Typing a few keys and hitting enter, he brought up another screen. "I'm going to put all the information in this system and have the computer generate your stunt."

Piper glanced at the screen. Some fields were already populated with numbers. "What are those?" she asked.

"Educated guesses, hypotheses. I used what I knew from my construction sites, but it won't replace the actual details the manufacturer, for instance, will be able to supply."

"This is very elaborate." Piper looked

closer. "Much more so than what I had on hand when we were building it."

"There were engineers there, right?" Cal asked.

"Sure. They sent me reports and probably did all the things you've done. I got an okay from them before we ran any tests and again on the day of the actual filming." She focused her attention on Cal. "I trust them. They'd been with us for years. I can't believe any one of them would want to sabotage the stunt, or my career, especially when Austin was inside the framework and at risk."

Cal's face was blank as he looked at her. She couldn't tell what he was thinking. Did he believe someone in the crew had intentionally caused the accident or set her up? Or set up Austin? Piper took a breath, silently answering her own question. Cal's scenario had never entered her mind.

"Breakfast!" Naomi stood in the doorway.

Both of them startled and looked up at her. Piper pushed her chair back and stood. At the same time, Cal did, too. They bumped into each other. He threw her off balance. Her hands flailed in the air, looking for something to hold on to. He caught her, pulling her to him. They intended to exit the small space behind the desk, but their movement had Cal holding her in his arms. Piper leaned into him, even though she knew she shouldn't. He smelled like a shower, fresh and clean, his soap a soft sandalwood fragrance.

Realizing where she was, Piper tried to move back, but the chair impeded her, and without Cal's hands holding her, she'd have fallen over.

"I'm sorry," she said, looking up at him. Something in his eyes made her voice catch in her throat and her hands tighten their grip on his arms.

As he pulled her level with him, neither said anything. She couldn't have spoken over the roar in her ears.

"Shall I serve breakfast—" Naomi's voice broke in "—or prepare a wedding cake?"

PIPER FELT HER face burn through her hairline all the way to the crown of her head. She dared not look at Cal. Whatever was in her mind had to be on her face and she knew he was astute enough to see it.

She turned toward the window, the direction she should have gone in the first place. Naomi had left by the time Piper was finally moving. Cal, judiciously, had turned away from her, but their eyes met as they approached the office exit.

"Don't mind her," he said. "She's been trying to get me interested in a little romance since I arrived." He smiled. "I'll bet she had something to say when she found you on the porch."

Piper nodded, unable to repeat Naomi's greeting.

"Let's eat. We have a lot of work to do and we need a meal," he said.

"What about your riding lesson? And I have a few lessons scheduled for today."

"That's right," he said as they took seats at the table where Naomi had placed silverware and coffee cups.

Piper noticed a bud vase with a yellow dandelion in it. She knew the older woman was doing that for her benefit. She couldn't see Cal sitting here each morning with a flower on his breakfast table.

Naomi set a plate in front of each of them and filled their coffee cups. She didn't ask if Piper wanted, liked or even drank coffee.

She knew Cal's preferences and probably remembered hers, too.

Cal took a bite of his toast and sipped his coffee as if everything was normal. Piper knew Naomi. At least she had known both her and her husband in the past. The woman could be sarcastic with her words, but her heart was good. Piper glanced at her, and instead of finding a frown, Naomi's eyes twinkled. She was hiding a smile.

"After breakfast, you should take care of your classes," Cal said. "I need to run a few errands anyway. I'll be back in time for my lesson."

"Sounds like a plan," she said.

Piper needed a plan. She also needed distance, but she felt Cal could help her. He might find something she hadn't been able to, after all.

"You're not hungry?" Cal asked.

Piper realized she'd been sitting there but not eating. Glancing down at her plate, she noticed the fried apples. They were her favorite. Naomi must have remembered that. Maybe that was what her smile was about. She took a bite. They were exactly as she remembered them. Piper closed her eyes, both from memory of past breakfasts and from the explosion of delicious tastes the simple fruit provided.

"Were these for me?" she asked Naomi when she could speak.

"For both of you. He likes them just as much as you do. That's the first thing I realized you two have in common."

Again, heat burned Piper's ears and fused into her face. Try as she might, she couldn't stop the furnace of feelings that seemed to grow within her each time Cal was near. She'd only come today because she couldn't sleep and was interested in knowing if he'd discovered anything.

She wasn't here for breakfast or for any other reason. She wasn't, she insisted to the internal voice in her head. But she couldn't be sure it was listening.

"Naomi, I know what you're trying to do," Cal said as soon as Piper finished her breakfast and left to return to her ranch and give her first lesson of the day.

Naomi was humming in the kitchen as she loaded the dishwasher and put things away.

"I'm not doing anything," she said, trying to conceal the grin that Cal could see.

"Strange how you're way too tall to even imitate cupid," he said. A head shorter than he was, Naomi stood straight-backed and commanding. In another life, he could see her as a drill sergeant, although one with a kind heart.

"Me?" She feigned surprise.

"You remember my time here is temporary, right?" Cal asked.

"I remember," she replied. But the way she said it told him she wasn't convinced.

Changing the subject, Cal said, "I'm going into town. Is there anything you need?"

Naomi picked up a paper from the counter and handed it to him. Cal scanned it. "You need these things?" The list had some of his favorite foods on it, but there were also items he'd never seen before.

"They're hers," Naomi supplied as if she could read his mind.

"Hers?"

"Don't act like you don't know who *she* is." Naomi raised her brows. "I'm sure we'll be seeing more of her before your *temporary* time here is over."

Cal saw the humor she was holding under the surface. He didn't think the comment was funny, but inside him, the thought of spending more time with Piper caused a jolt of pleasure. He put the list in his shirt pocket and left. Naomi wasn't laughing out loud, but he could hear her as if she was.

It wasn't thoughts of Naomi that followed him into his truck and all the way to town. It was the brown-eyed woman who had sneaked into his dreams. Their accidental bump had put her in his arms, giving him a glimpse of the way they fit together and a promise of something he didn't know was missing in his life.

But obviously Naomi did or thought she did.

THE DRIVE INTO Waymon Valley was generally short, but today Cal took his time. He didn't want to race to get anywhere. He needed time to digest what was going on inside him. He thought he'd have hours last night, but once he started looking at Piper's video, his mind had been consumed with trying to decipher it. When he went to bed, he fell right asleep, but his dreams were full of her and time spent with her and their horses.

He should have awakened tired from the day's exercise, but he felt refreshed. When Piper appeared in the office doorway, it was all he could do not to act like a fool. Yet he couldn't stop the pleasure he felt at seeing her. He wasn't sure if she saw it, sensed it.

Cal had reached town and as usual the waves and smiles of people on the street garnered his attention. Waymon Valley retained the feel of an old west town. Red or tan brick buildings lined the downtown streets. Miss Rita's Dance Studio sat next to the barbershop. Across the street, tucked between the fire house and a bookstore was the diner where he'd had dinner with Piper. Passing these shops and businesses, Cal parked in the grocery store lot. Stepping down from his truck, and with a quick wave to a total stranger, he went inside.

The store today had no trace of Piper. She was giving a lesson. Going up and down the aisles, he selected the items from Naomi's list, putting them one by one in his cart. Selecting the apples from the produce section, he thought of Piper again and her surprise at the breakfast entrée. Her face had gone red when Naomi had joked and her comment openly connected the two of them.

Cal should have been embarrassed, but he wasn't. He didn't have any bad feeling. Seeing Piper beside him at his desk had conjured feelings he hadn't known he had. For the second time recently, he thought of his brother and Lauren. Had they begun with feelings like this? Cal shook his head. He needed to stay focused.

Checking the list again, Cal pulled his attention back to the store. He picked up a box of Belgian waffle mix. It was a brand he'd never seen before, but Naomi's precise handwriting had noted it. He hadn't had a Belgian waffle in ages, and even though he'd eaten less than an hour ago, the smell of the sugar through the package made him yearn for the sweet bread. Placing it in the cart, he found the rest of the listed items. Finally, he had everything Naomi needed and a few treats of his own.

After storing the bags in his truck, he walked down the street and entered the hotel. There was only one person he was interested in and that was Meghan Evans. He didn't see her until his eyes became accustomed to the dim light.

"Cal," Meghan said with a smile. "How can I help you?"

"I'm taking riding lessons."

"Is that a fact?" she said, her eyes widening. "I suppose Piper is the teacher."

He didn't have to answer. The look on her face told him she knew the truth.

"I need proper riding clothes, boots, maybe a hat. Could you point me to a place where I can get that?"

"I'd be happy to. Since Piper started that school, there's been a demand for riding gear."

"Oh," Cal said.

"That's what Pete Gallagher told me. He owns the outfitter store."

Cal said nothing. He waited for her to continue.

"The store is called Gallagher's Western Clothing. It's about a mile down Main Street.

There's a huge white buffalo in front of it. So it'll be hard to miss."

"Aren't there any other riding schools in the area?"

"Plenty of them, but none run by a former famous stuntwoman."

"I see," Cal said.

Before he could turn to leave, Meghan asked another question. "How are the lessons going by the way?"

"Let's just say my contact with the ground is decreasing."

Meghan laughed. "Piper is a good teacher. She'll have you turning cartwheels on horseback in no time."

"That remains to be seen," Cal said. At the door, he waved goodbye and returned to the truck.

The store wasn't busy when he entered it several minutes later, but there were a few customers inside. As usual they smiled when he passed them. Checking the racks of riding pants, he selected a few and tried them on. He needed boots and Gallagher's proved to have a vast number of styles and colors.

"He's the one," he heard someone whisper.

Cal didn't look in the direction the voice

had come from. He stood up to check the boots and overheard another whispered comment.

"He's on the ranch next to the Hollywood woman. You know the one."

He turned toward them. Immediately, they averted their eyes.

He finally understood Piper's comment about the rumors in town.

When he left Gallagher's Western Clothing, he had plenty of riding clothes and a new pair of boots. He'd come to Montana with only a few things and never needed a huge wardrobe anyway. The shopping took longer than he expected, however, and he was ready to head back to the ranch. Passing the diner made him think of the talk about Piper. Cal decided to get a coffee before leaving.

The diner was quiet. Only a few people occupied the tables and counter. They smiled and nodded when he walked by. Hooking a leg over a stool, he sat down. Diner owner Ally was watching the big-screen television that hung from the ceiling at one end of the counter. There was an action scene going on. Cal was unfamiliar with the movie, but he knew enough to recognize a major turning point when he saw one.

"Mr. Masters," she greeted him. "How's it going?"

"Fine, thanks."

"Have you decided what you're going to do with the ranch?"

"Do?" he questioned.

She looked as if she'd spoken out of turn.

"I'm sorry," Cal said. "I hadn't really thought of doing anything. I'm not planning to stay in Waymon Valley."

"I didn't know," she said.

"I understand. I only came here for a visit and some relaxation. The horses are great for that. I'm an engineer and I need to get back to it soon."

"Well, we'll be sorry to see you go. Whenever that is," she added. "Now, what can I get you?"

"Coffee, to go," he said when she looked at him. "Black. And maybe a piece of that cake." He indicated the cake under a glass dome on the counter.

She smiled and picked up the pot and filled a cup, then added a lid. Cal's eyes were on the flat-screen television as she passed the cup to him.

"You like action movies, I take it," he said conversationally.

"Not really. I'm more the romance story type, along with tearjerkers. I'm a sucker for a good cry," Ally said, now cutting a piece of cake for him.

Cal placed money on the counter, indicating that he needed no change.

"If Piper wasn't in this one, I'd probably skip it."

"Piper?" Cal's head came up and he looked closely at the screen. "Piper's acting?"

"She's a stuntwoman. She does all the stunts for Elisabeth Grey."

Sure, Cal didn't see many movies, since he moved around a lot, but even he knew of Elisabeth Grey—young, beautiful, great actress and a wonderful humanitarian.

"Piper doubles for her?" His attention was still on the screen. He knew Piper had worked on films, but he hadn't made the connection that she would be such a star, or performing in place of one.

"Did." Ally drew his attention now. "She

hasn't worked since she returned to the ranch a year ago. No one knows why, but…" Ally leaned forward and lowered her voice. "I think it had something to do with that accident."

She closed one eye. It wasn't exactly a wink, more like a confirmation. Before Cal could respond, she'd moved along the counter to take care of another customer. He picked up his coffee and slice of cake, and left the diner. Piper Logan doubled for Elisabeth Grey.

Of course, he knew about the accident. He was actively working on how it might have happened. A thought came to him as he slipped into the truck's seat. Any accident on a site required an incident report. Something as important as a person being hurt had to have involved the police or other authorities. He wondered if Piper had the documentation.

On the other hand, he'd get the report, but not from her. That accident was a nightmare for Piper and she was still living it. The report was public record, he'd bet. He'd access it online and read the account. Cal didn't know exactly what he was looking for. At this point it was too early to tell. But he knew he wanted her to be whole again and find her lost spirit.

CHAPTER SIX

WHEN THE HOTEL EMILY was built in the early twentieth century, the railroad bisected the town of Waymon Valley. Meghan's forward-thinking ancestor, the hotel's namesake, insisted that both the front and back entrances be equally majestic. And now that the small town sprawled wider, the Emily was part of a downtown area with a city hall, a sheriff's office, and stores and services. The streets may see cars and trucks, but it was still a down-to-earth Western town.

Piper drove past the hotel to the large house located on its east side. It looked like an addition, but in fact, it was the original boardinghouse that once provided lodgings for miners and was now the sole residence of Meghan Evans.

From the parked cars and trucks in front, it appeared the gang was all here, she thought, likening them to the horde of Hollywood paparazzi that dogged her after the accident.

Getting down from the cab, Piper closed the truck door and stood looking at the old home with its thoroughly modern transformation.

Taking a deep breath, she knew she couldn't put it off any longer. Time to run the gauntlet. When Meghan opened the door, Piper's smile was in place. They hugged as usual and Meghan pulled her inside.

"Relax," she whispered. "No one is here to bite you."

"No, just to goggle at me—and wonder."

Piper hadn't taken three steps into the main room before she was approached by a very tall man.

"Hello," he said with an outstretched hand. Piper took it.

"This is Sam Winslow. He owns one of the shops. They do wedding photos, school pictures, baby announcements and everything related to photography."

"From learning to use your basic camera to etching scenes on glass or acrylics," Sam added.

"And he will talk your ear off," Meghan

added. "So let her meet some of the other people before you try to monopolize her," Meghan said and winked.

Sam smiled and dropped Piper's hand.

"It's a pleasure to meet you, Sam," Piper said.

She moved away, ready for the stares and the questions. What she got was a bear hug. Piper didn't get to see the face of the man who was suddenly holding her tight enough to cut off her breathing.

She pushed back and looked up.

"Piper, how's my girl?" The bellow could be heard all the way to the kitchen.

"Mark? Mark Jackson?"

"The one and only. We've missed you around here." He hugged her again.

Mark was six foot four in his stocking feet. He appeared even taller than Piper remembered. She wasn't his girl, had never been his girl, but they were friends.

"What are you doing now?" she asked. "I thought you'd left Waymon Valley."

"I did. Lived in Seattle for a few years, but missed home, missed the mountains. I took over my dad's practice. I work at the hospital now."

"That's great." Piper didn't feel any eyes on her that weren't admiring or friendly. She recognized a few of the people, but most were new to her. Everyone seemed to own something in town or work on one of the ranches in the area.

There was one woman with her husband who looked familiar. Piper didn't know where she'd seen her before, but she was sure she had. She caught Piper staring at her and started toward her. Her smile was wide and genuine, and she was clearly the most beautiful woman in the room.

"I'm Rosa Clayton. My husband is Adam Osborne." She looked over her shoulder at a tall man, average build, nice features. He was grinning at Rosa from ear to ear.

Piper thought they made a sweet couple. She could tell they were in love.

"You look very familiar," Piper said. "I thought I might have met you before."

Rosa shook her head. "I was never in the movies," she said. "I used to be a model, some commercials."

"That's it." Piper remembered. "You were in cosmetics ads. The face of the Darling brand." Piper could see her in the television spots, putting on her lipstick or applying blush across her high cheekbones.

She nodded. "I modeled for them for years."

"And the evening gowns, along with the diamonds. I loved the way you flourished through that door in the commercials."

Piper almost turned around showing her what she meant. She felt she'd met a kindred spirit.

After a while, Piper completely relaxed. Just as Meghan said, no one was there to bring up Piper's past. She moved about the room, talking to the other guests and having a good time.

Then the door opened and Cal came in. Piper's heart lifted. She was glad to see him and it had to show on her face. Without thinking, she went toward him. If Mark hadn't stepped in front of him before she got close enough, she was sure she'd have gone straight into his arms. As it was, the two men were shaking hands when she stopped.

Mark stepped aside and Cal looked at Piper. "I guess you don't need rescuing," he said.

"You're here to rescue me?"

"If things weren't going well, I'd put you on my white steed and carry you to safety."

She laughed. "You don't have a white horse, or even a white truck."

"I was being metaphorical."

They began to stroll into the room.

"You know, I've driven by this place several times," he said. "I thought this was part of the hotel."

"Originally, it *was* the hotel."

"Really?"

Cal looked up at the ceiling.

"It was a boardinghouse. Meghan's aunt built it. Well, several great-aunt versions back. I can't remember how many. It's been remodeled several times. One of Meghan's past relatives apparently had a large family, so he converted it into a single-family home back in the 1940s and opened the hotel separately. It's been that way ever since."

They had reached the bar and Cal handed her a fresh glass of wine. Rosa came over and introduced her husband. Just as Cal was shaking hands, Piper heard her name called. The entire room looked at the speaker, including her and Cal.

Piper recognized the newest guest, but

her name eluded her for a moment. Shelby...
Shelby Chase, she remembered. They'd been
dressage competitors back in junior high
school.

By the expression on Meghan's face, Piper
knew her friend was surprised to see Shelby.
Piper had won their final competition and
Shelby had never forgiven her.

Quickly, Piper tried to think of a way to
greet the woman, for Shelby Chase rarely
went anywhere unless she was the center of
attention. Tonight, Piper was sure it would
be her turn to suffer Shelby's wrath. Cal
put his hand on Piper's elbow. She glanced
at him, giving him a reassuring smile, and
left to confront Shelby.

Setting her glass on the bar, she walked
across the room feeling as if she were heading into the lion's den. But she was Hollywood trained. She'd been taught by the best
how to assess a situation and defuse it. So
she went on the offense.

"Shelby," she said, smiling her best smile.
"Great to see you again." Piper kissed the air
about them, a gesture that was right in between being a friend or an enemy. And Piper
knew exactly which category she and Shelby

fit in. Standing back, she admired her former competitor. Her dress was an attention-getting red and it didn't fail to define all her curves. "That dress was made for you."

"I know," Shelby drawled. "No one else could carry this off as well as I can." She twirled around, giving the full effect of the fancy garment.

As humble as ever, Piper thought sarcastically.

"Still riding?" Piper asked, leading her to a tray with glasses of sparkling water. The room seemed to have lost interest in them, although Piper was willing to bet large that Cal and Meghan were following their movements with interest.

"I have a school. My students compete. We have cases of blue ribbons and trophies."

"That's wonderful. I'm glad to hear it. You were always an excellent horsewoman." That part was true.

Shelby smiled or smirked, Piper couldn't tell which one, as the other woman took pride in herself. Piper couldn't believe Shelby was the same selfish person she'd been in high school. Her saving grace was horses. She *was* an excellent horsewoman.

Piper had seen that trophy case Shelby had and it was full of ribbons and awards. So, Piper had to concede that Shelby was a fine teacher or at least effective at hiring teachers.

"I see you've posted a flyer to get clients for your start-up business. I spotted it in the grocery store, but I hear you have them in the library, bookstore, Gallaghers, all over town."

"I have," Piper acknowledged. She recognized the insult in that. She chose to ignore it, even though her teeth were on edge. "I have a few students who are doing well."

Shelby lifted a shoulder as if dismissing the accomplishment.

"I even have one student who's learning trick riding."

Her brows went up.

"Are you going to be here long enough to make any headway in that type of teaching?"

Her question already had her answering it in the negative.

"He's doing quite well. I might add that to my list of services. I'm sure graduates of the program can go further at competitions than the standard."

"I don't know of any competitions for trick riding," Shelby said.

"I suppose not. Your students excel in dressage and jumping." Piper let her annoyance creep into her voice.

Shelby's face turned as red as her gown.

"You know, Piper," Shelby whispered. "You being from Hollywood and all, I thought you'd dress better." She used a couple of fingers to pick invisible lint from Piper's shoulder.

"That's all you've got, Shelby? To change the subject because someone gets the upper hand on you?"

"Well, it's true." Shelby's tone was smug.

Piper knew better than to take the bait. She'd been on a world stage with cameras and microphones thrust in her face as she tried to get through a crowd.

"There are places to wear Dior dresses and places to tone it down a bit," Piper said. She looked Shelby up and down for several seconds. "Your dress says you're looking for something. Mine says I've confidently found it."

Unintentionally, she glanced over her shoulder at Cal. She hadn't decided to do that. It just came naturally.

"I see," Shelby said. "Is he a stuntman, too?"

"He's an engineer. He bought the Christensen ranch. I thought you'd heard."

Shelby gave a nod. "I guess you should give up the trick riding stuff, though, and move on to some other profession. Maybe next time you won't get anyone hurt."

And there it was, Piper thought. The subject that Shelby had come here to draw out. And likely make a scene on purpose.

"Is there a problem here?" Meghan had come over when Shelby's voice became a stage whisper.

"You seem to have a question about me," Cal said.

He joined the small group, standing at Piper's side. The three of them blocked anyone behind them from seeing.

Shelby retreated. "We were just having a pleasant conversation."

"I don't think so," Meghan said. "I didn't invite you, Shelby. As this is my home, I suggest you pull your claws in and be a good guest. I'd hate to have to ask you to leave in front of all these people."

Shelby hesitated. She looked from face to face. Piper wondered if she was deciding if Meghan was serious or not. Finally, she laughed. "You all are pushing this way out of proportion. Piper and I were just having a good ol' chat. The way we've done for years. Right, Piper?"

"Right," Piper said. It was the way they had spoken for years. The two women stared at each other. Shelby suddenly turned and with a flourish was gone. Then Piper turned. "Meghan, I apologize for this."

"It wasn't your fault," Meghan said. "Please, stay and enjoy. I know the Mervais twins haven't had a chance to talk to you yet and they'd really like to."

She nodded and Cal led her back to the party, his arm around her. The room had become quiet, as people instinctively knew something was going on. Unwilling to acknowledge their stares, she and Cal immediately began to speak to someone close by.

Piper trembled at the thought of what folks were saying about her. She wanted to believe things would be different, but the underlying vibe of the room was as loud as if people were shouting. She tightened her grip on Cal's waist. When she made eye contact with someone, they quickly dropped their gaze.

"I knew this would happen," she whispered so only Cal could hear her.

"Don't judge so quickly," he said.

Suddenly he was heading for a group of people in one corner of the room. Piper knew them. Cal tugged her along, and unless she wanted to create another scene, she had to keep walking.

One of the guys looked up, seeing their approach. It was Pete Gallagher. Piper had gone to school with him since the first grade. "Piper, Cal," Pete said, shaking Cal's hand. "It's great to see you again." He directed this comment to Piper.

She nodded and tried to smile.

"Don't believe anything Shelby says. You know she's been jealous of you since we were kids," Pete advised.

His words made her relax a little.

"And thanks for throwing business my way." Pete glanced at Cal.

"I'm still breaking in the boots," Cal said.

"I imagine I might need more pants if the ground has anything to do with it."

Pete laughed.

A couple came up and joined them. "Let me introduce you to Joan and Maxwell Campbell," Pete said. "They are both teachers."

"Call me Max."

Pete introduced Cal and told a little about Piper's work in Hollywood.

"But we're glad to have her back in the Valley," he finished.

"I've watched a number of your movies," Joan said.

"You have?" Piper didn't mean to sound so surprised, but no one really knew which movies she was in. Her face was never on the screen, and if it was, she'd been made up to look like the actor or actress she was standing in for.

"You can't live in the Valley and not know about you," Max said.

Piper stiffened. She could take that one of two ways—as the revered hometown girl does good or as the notorious stunt coordinator who nearly got a man killed. In any case, she was done with trying to hide from it.

"I realize there is an elephant in the room," Piper said. "An elephant that's getting larger by the minute."

She looked at Cal. His eyes told her she didn't have to do this.

"I do," she said, answering his silent comment. Facing Pete, Max, Joan and the others in her small circle, she said, "I was in charge of the stunt when there was an accident."

The room grew quiet. Every eye was on her. But she was going forward from now on.

"I'm sure you're all curious about what happened. Did I really do something wrong like all the news reports said?"

People moved closer to her, pressing in to hear better. Piper moved back, allowing the circle to widen.

"The truth is, I don't know. That sounds like an excuse." She went on to explain that she was still looking into the circumstances.

"Do you think you'll find anything?" Pete asked.

"I don't know."

"But I'll be helping her," Cal said.

"Is there anything we can do to help?" Adam Osborne asked.

Piper was surprised. They were accepting her without any accusing questions.

"Not yet," Piper said.

"But after a little more investigation," Cal joined in. "We might need a lot of help."

"You can count on me," Meghan said.

Piper smiled, knowing her friend would always be on her side. Then came a round of supportive comments.

Piper relaxed totally. Conversation eased from subject to subject, mainly local politics, the weather and the next stock auction. People moved in and out of groups while Cal kept close to her side. She would have felt that he was trying to make a statement that they were a couple, but she wanted his attention and his strength.

She'd never felt the need for a protector, but after the relentless press coverage and defection of some of her friends after the accident, her faith in herself had been shaken. Tonight, she'd gotten a little of it back.

The rest of the night went well. She almost forgot the disagreeable scene between herself and Shelby.

By midnight, people had begun to drift away. Piper should be ready to leave, but she was riding on some kind of high she hadn't felt for over a year.

"Let me help you clean up," she told Meghan when the last of the guests left with happy smiles and thank-yous. Only she and Cal remained. She picked up two candy dishes and headed for the kitchen.

"Me, too," Cal added.

"You've done enough. I can get this. There isn't much anyway. So, you go home. You must be tired."

She was, but it was a happy kind of tired. Even though Piper had fun and enjoyed herself, the relief of people being in her corner was unexpected and seemed to remove an invisible weight from her shoulders. The loss of it, however, had a weight of its own.

"Go on," Meghan said. "You've got a long day tomorrow. You need some sleep."

"Are you sure?" Piper asked. She did have a long day coming, but Meghan didn't know that.

"I'm sure. Cal, make sure she gets home safe."

"I will," he said.

True to his word, Cal followed her all the way to her porch stairs. Piper wanted to rush up the steps and go inside, but just like on that first day in the gym, tonight Cal had been her rock. She'd brightened when he came through the door at Meghan's party. It had been good to see a familiar face, even if they'd only met recently. Plus, he'd squired her around Meghan's room, letting her know with the touch of his hand on her back that he was there for her. Ignoring him now would be more than rude.

She headed for his truck. He was still behind the wheel, but he got out as she started toward him.

"Thanks," she said, realizing this was the first time tonight they had been alone. The air had cooled and a gentle breeze blew from the west, but Piper felt warm.

"For what?" Cal asked.

"For coming to rescue me."

"Even though you didn't need it," he reminded her.

"For standing by me when Shelby began her assault."

"I was only there for moral support. You had the situation well in hand."

"For not judging me." Piper knew that was the most important thing he'd done. Not at the party, but also on the ranch. He'd given her the benefit of explaining herself instead of just agreeing with all the media and industry types that placed the blame on her.

"Good night," she said.

She stepped back but paused. Cal took her hand and pulled her forward. He leaned in to kiss her on the cheek. Why Piper turned her head, she didn't know, but his mouth landed on hers. He quickly lifted his head in surprise.

"Good night," she said and pushed herself away.

"See you tomorrow," he added.

"You mean today." She laughed to cover her nervousness. Why had she turned into his kiss? She wanted to put her hands on her cheeks. She knew they were flaming if the heat in her ears was any indication of what her face looked like.

For a moment, she was unable to decide what to do. All her confidence fled. The sound of Cal opening the truck's door snapped her out of her thoughts and she backed up, giving them both more room.

"Thanks again," she said.

"Thank *you*," he responded.

Piper's eyes met Cal's. It was his tone that caught her. He was thanking her for the kiss, for the way she reacted to him. That hadn't been acting. A lump rose in her throat. Piper took another step back. She knew if she didn't, she'd rush back into those strong arms.

And neither of them were ready for that. At least she didn't think so, but that kiss, however brief, said something different. She wasn't sure what Cal thought and her mind was still in a jumble.

But something in her had changed.

IT COULDN'T BE time to get up yet, Piper thought as the ringing of her phone penetrated her brain. She'd been up half the night after Cal left. Their kiss was on the top of her mind and refused to relinquish it to sleep.

Keeping her eyes closed, she groaned at the sound. Groping for the phone, she pulled it up to her face. Peering through one eye, she saw Meghan's face on the display.

"Hullo," she said, shifting away from the sunlight glaring through the curtains.

"Did I wake you?" Meghan asked.

"You know you did," she said. "Couldn't you have waited until noon or later?"

"This is Montana, not California. Our clocks start when the chickens wake up."

"You haven't seen a chicken in years that wasn't already cut and cooked. So, what do you want to know?"

Piper pushed the covers aside and sat up, resting against the cushioned headboard of her bed. She still refused to open her eyes.

"Are you okay?"

"You mean after Shelby. Yes, I'm okay. Shelby has tried to sabotage me for years. I can handle her."

"Good. I was glad she took my hint when I asked her to leave. And your speech certainly took all the wind out of her sails, or venom out of her mouth," Meghan said. "Last I saw, she was on the sidewalk chatting to Mark."

"Dr. Mark?" Piper said. "He's always been a friend of mine."

"You mean he wants to be more than a friend."

"He doesn't." Her eyes finally opened wide.

"Oh, give me a break. You had to know that. He never made a secret of it," Meghan said.

"He's over that, Meghan. Mark is married—with children."

"You never forget your first love."

"Are we going to talk about Carter Richardson?"

"No, we are not." Meghan's voice was emphatic. Carter had been her first love. He transferred to Waymon Valley in the fourth grade and Meghan had followed him around nonstop.

"Speaking of first loves and such, how's Mr. Masters? He didn't seem to be running from you last night."

"He did as you asked, too, and saw me all the way to my door."

"Anything happen at the door?"

Piper could hear the hopefulness in her voice.

"What are you, the unofficial town matchmaker? Because I think you need a license to do it professionally." Piper's face was warm again. The mere mention of Cal's name affected her. Thankfully, Meghan couldn't see her or there'd be more to this conversation.

"I'm the official friend."

"Well, what do you want at this hour of the morning, official friend?"

"Just to make sure you got home safely and that Cal didn't make any moves on you."

"And what if he had?" Piper asked.

"What!" Meghan all but shouted.

Piper held the cell away from her ear.

"Did he?"

"Not exactly," she hedged.

"What does that mean?"

"All right, if you must know, he kissed me." Or I kissed him, Piper thought. She wasn't sure. They had both leaned in together. Still, she didn't know why she had done it. She could make up reasons, but none of them fit and none were the truth.

"Did you kiss him back?" Meghan broke into her thoughts.

"It was too brief an encounter to say."

Meghan whooped and shouted on the other end of the line. Piper moved the phone farther away from her ear until the happiness stopped.

"But we may as well stop, whatever it is," Piper said. "Cal has already mentioned he's leaving the Valley. Job offers are already coming in. So there's no need for me to start a relationship with someone who won't be around. And I won't be around, either, if you recall."

"Piper, you need to get past what happened with Xavier."

"I am past him," Piper said.

"All right." Meghan backed off. "But if Cal kisses you again, be sure to kiss him back. Now, gotta go. See ya!"

Meghan hung up then, not giving Piper time for a reply and leaving her with the image of being in Cal's arms, his mouth pressing deliciously on hers.

THE DOORBELL RANG before Piper was ready. Jumping out of bed, she ran one way and then the other, not able to decide what to do first. It was Cal at the door. It was time for them to begin work.

She could hear him calling to her but only heard the word *cake*. The rest of his message was muffled.

"I'll be down in a minute," she shouted, unsure if he could hear her. Dressing as fast as she could, she pulled a shirt and jeans on. Then running down the stairs, she yanked the door open.

Cal stood with his back to her.

"Sorry," she said breathlessly. "I overslept." She pushed a hand through her unkempt hair. "I would say help yourself to coffee, but I didn't make any. So, take a seat. I'll be right back."

She ran up the stairs, quickly rushing through her morning routine. Seven minutes later when she returned to the living room, Cal wasn't there. She found him in the kitchen standing before the wall of windows drinking a cup of coffee.

"I made it," he said. "Yours is there."

He pointed toward the counter and Piper followed his gaze. Lifting the cup, she took a sip. It was perfect.

"Meghan called and kept me on the phone." It was the total truth, but she wasn't going into the fact that she'd relived their kiss until it was almost morning.

"Did she want to know if I kissed you good-night?"

Piper practically dropped her cup. She set it on the counter with a thud. "How did you know?"

Cal laughed and faced her. "Don't you think I can spot matchmaking when I see it?"

"As a matter of fact, no."

He shook his head as if wiping the comment aside.

"What did you tell her?"

"The truth."

"The truth has many versions," Cal said. "Did you tell her the whole and unvarnished truth?"

Piper shook her head. "Only we should know that."

"We're not going to let it interfere with our project, right?"

"There's no reason we should," Piper said. "However, I want to apologize…"

"Don't." Cal gestured and she stopped talking. "Let's just leave it," he said.

"Leave it?"

"We have different lives and different goals. You want to return to California and who knows where my job will take me."

"It's better if we just forget it ever happened."

"I think that's the best option."

Piper nodded. She should say something, but there were no words. They should go to work, get on with his lesson, but she had no heart for it. She needed time to think, to process what had just gone on in this kitchen.

She needed to decide what she thought about that kiss. It didn't bind them to each other. Yet it was something. And she wanted Cal to say it meant something to him.

But he wanted to *just* leave it. That was for the best, she told herself. They both had agreed on that. And they knew that a relationship was out of the question. Piper would do better with one of the single men who lived in the Valley and had no wish to leave it. Cal had no wish to stay. Neither did she. Not under the circumstances.

If he could just leave it, so could she. She repeated this silently over and over. But somehow she didn't believe it.

CHAPTER SEVEN

TAMARA ST. JOHN was not well-known outside of a Hollywood film set. She was a pretty face, a beautiful face, and talented in many ways. Working in an industry that valued these traits, she stood out, and that was saying something. In street clothes, with little makeup on and her hair fluttering around her shoulders, she was simply Piper's friend. And Piper was expecting a delivery from her.

Riding Silver, Piper galloped to the mailbox on top of a short post at the edge of the ranch. The envelope was there. Not waiting to return to the house, she slid it open and pulled out the photos.

She smiled a silent thank-you to her absent friend. The stills were from *The Diamond Affair*, the movie where Piper's stunt went wrong.

CAL WAS IN his office as soon as his boots hit the hardwood floor in the house. He dropped two bags of groceries on the kitchen counter and continued straight to his computer, not even saying a word to Naomi. He wheeled his office chair closer to the machine.

"You okay?" Naomi asked from the doorway.

Cal didn't look up. He watched the screen flicker through the self-check process.

"I just got an idea I need to act on," he told her.

He could hear that Naomi had not moved.

"I'm all right," he told her, looking up for the first time.

Naomi stopped drying her hands on the towel she held and gave him her signature look, at least that was what Cal thought of it as. Short of putting her hands on her hips, she lowered her chin and stared at him as if she could read his mind. A second later, probably deciding he was telling the truth, Naomi slung the towel over her shoulder and, with a concerning glance, returned to the kitchen.

Typing in his password, Cal searched for Piper Logan on one of the movie databases. It had a bio and all the credits for films she'd been part of. None that he checked had her as the stunt coordinator. He assumed the film where the accident occurred was either not completed or never released.

Checking further, he found a newspaper article about the accident. The film was *The Diamond Affair*. When he opened the link and read he found that the stunt coordinator was Xavier Fabriano. Irrationally, Cal disliked the man.

He went on reading and searching, spending his time trying to piece together the accident and learning what he could about his beautiful neighbor. He spent an hour combing through the logistics of the stunt, every detail he could find. At the end he still had a gut feeling that Piper hadn't done anything wrong. Her crusading spirit told him she was convinced that she was missing something to explain the accident. And he was sure she'd spend her life trying to find it.

Switching computer programs, Cal took the information Piper had given him and began doing more calculations. He didn't think of the time. He hardly noticed Naomi popping in and out with food and drink. He was totally absorbed in his task.

"You better take a real break," Naomi said

the last time she put a tray next to him. "Or your legs will go to sleep and you won't be able to walk—or ride."

"Ride!"

Her last two words held special emphasis and a double meaning. Still, Cal knew she was right. He needed to stand up and do something physical. He could always return later on. Cal had already had his riding lesson. Going to exercise his horses would just bring him in contact with Piper. Cal smiled at the thought of that. He wasn't a jogger, and while there was no swimming pool on the grounds, he did like to swim. There was a fitness center in town, but it had no pool. Maybe he'd see if the hotel had a program that would give him access to their pool.

Cal stretched, feeling his muscles protest from sitting in the same position too long. He did need to exercise. Half an hour later, he was in the hotel pool. Thirty minutes after that, he'd completed fifty laps. The water felt good and Cal was invigorated as he pulled his long body out of the pool. Grabbing his towel, he dried enough of the dripping water to return to the locker room, where he showered and dressed.

"How was it?" Meghan asked as he emerged into the hotel lobby. Cal met her near one of the oversize wing-backed chairs that were large enough for two people to sit comfortably in.

"It was worth the drive," he said.

"Well, you're welcome to use it anytime. Although, when there's a rodeo nearby, the spillover usually fills this place up and the kids love the pool."

"I'll make a note of that."

"How's the stunt riding lessons going?" Meghan asked. Obviously, Piper had related that information to her.

"Piper is an exceptional teacher."

"True, we learned to ride together."

"I didn't know that," Cal said. "Do you do stunts, too?"

Meghan shook her head. "That's strictly Piper. She's the adventurous one."

"I guess so," Cal said. "Considering the profession she chose."

Meghan laughed. "I never thought of it like that. She's so conscious of safety."

"I've noticed," Cal told her.

Meghan's attention moved from him to something over his shoulder. Cal started to turn.

"Well, speaking of," she said.

Piper was walking toward Meghan, but seeing him, she stopped, her expression perplexed.

"Cal, I didn't expect to see you," she said when her feet finally moved and she came within speaking distance.

"Thought I'd go for a swim and Meghan kindly allowed me to use the hotel pool."

"What are you doing here, Piper?" Meghan asked. "Is anything wrong?"

"Nothing like that. One of my students needed a ride home and I agreed to drop her off. While here, I thought I'd come say hello."

Cal thought it was more than that. She probably wanted to speak to her friend without others around, without *him* around.

"I'll leave you two to your conversation," he said. "Thanks again, Meghan. For the use of the pool," he added.

He was two steps away when he heard Meghan. "Don't leave," she said.

Cal stopped and looked over his shoulder.

"I have something to get done. It can't wait. Why don't you and Piper have some coffee and I'll join you as soon as I finish?"

Cal didn't see Piper move. The fact that she didn't turn to look at him told him she was glaring at her friend.

"Piper, is that all right with you?" He couldn't help teasing her. From the beginning, he'd shown up in places that seemed to thwart her. "Maybe we could have cake with the coffee."

At that, she turned to him. "Cake," she said. "Of course, what is coffee without cake?"

He didn't think Meghan knew anything about the private joke between Piper and himself. But she knew about his stunt riding lessons. So maybe the cake was also something Piper had shared.

"I'll meet you in the coffee shop in half an hour," Meghan said. Taking a couple of steps back, she gave them both a look and moved on toward her office.

"You really don't have to have coffee with me," Cal told Piper. "I recognize Meghan's setup and I understand that you came here to talk to her, not me."

When she didn't respond, he continued.

"I'm flexible. I can spare a few minutes," Cal said. "Is something wrong?"

"You were in the pool," she stated, seeming to change the subject.

"Naomi said I needed some exercise. I'd been at my computer too long."

She gave a curt nod but didn't say anything more. When she began to walk, he walked with her.

"Oh, before I forget, I e-mailed you most of the information you asked me for."

"Thanks."

In the coffee shop, they found seats. Cal ordered coffee and cake from the counter and brought it over.

"I got chocolate for us because I've only ever met one person in the world who didn't like chocolate."

"That wouldn't be me," she said, accepting the cup and the hunk of cake.

"And one other person who doesn't eat carbs," he teased, looking at the cake.

"So how was your swim?" she asked, ignoring him.

"It did the trick. I feel a lot better now. For a hotel pool, it's a good size."

"For a long while, it was the only one in

the area and it was small. That one is inside. The large one is outside. I assume that's the one you used."

Nodding, he said, "It's great for swimming laps."

"Is that something you did while on engineering sites?" She took a bite of her cake.

"Every chance I got. Often, not always, it was in a lake or a river. What about you? Along with horseback riding and gymnastics, is swimming also one of your skills?"

"On a set, I've been known to swim. For me, it was often the ocean."

"What about pleasure? Don't you do anything just for you?"

It was a question she couldn't remember ever being asked. "As you know, I love what I do…did," she corrected. "For pleasure, I'd read, play tennis, ride horses."

"Tennis is technically work if you ever played it in a movie. Plus, it's also conditioning for the stunts you have to be strong enough to do."

"You could say that of everything under the sun, even reading."

Cal agreed with her. "How about skydiving, windsurfing, zip lining?"

"Done them all."

"Wow, you'd be a hard date," Cal said.

"Date?" She picked up on the word.

"It would be hard to decide where to take you. You've done everything and probably have to be very good at them all."

"Not that I'm dating," Piper emphasized. "But I've never built a road or bridge or pipeline."

Cal smiled. "Those aren't exactly recreational activities."

"There's always dinner and a movie, or don't people do that anymore?" she asked.

"Seems very *normal*."

Piper smiled. She held back the laugh that bubbled up inside her. "What? You were thinking of something *abnormal*?" she teased.

"Outside the box," Cal said. "I figured you wouldn't want to do the normal thing."

"Why not?" She feigned hurt. "Do I appear to be someone who needs to be wonderfully surprised on a date?"

"Exactly," he said.

"Date? Did I hear that you two are planning a date?" Meghan slipped into the chair next to Piper.

"No," they both said in unison.

DID HE REALLY want to date her? Cal asked himself that question several times on the drive back to the ranch. The idea wasn't totally foreign to him. He must have thought about it subconsciously. Piper was an amazing woman and he hadn't dated anyone seriously in a long time. Not that he was looking for a serious relationship. She was his neighbor, his trainer, an interesting person and someone with serious goals of her own.

Meanwhile, he'd be off on another job soon. He'd already had offers, two of which he'd agreed to discuss the requirements for. One was in Central America and the other in Africa. Cal should be preparing for those conversations, but Piper was on his mind. He couldn't seem to relegate her to a safe place in his thoughts.

At some point, Cal decided to see one of the films she was in. He'd only watched a few minutes of the one playing in the diner. Signing on to a streaming service, he brought up a list of movies where Piper was a stuntwoman. As the sun set, he sat comfortably in the house's media room and started the first one he'd chosen. Seeing her doing the stunts had him on edge even more than the nature of the story. It didn't matter that he knew she was safe at her ranch a few miles away or with Meghan in town. That knowledge didn't keep him from being on the edge of his seat.

Dropping his shoulders as the movie ended, Cal was unaware how tight his body had become as he viewed the big screen. Automatically, the second movie started. It opened with an action scene that immediately grabbed his attention, and he watched half of it before pausing the film and getting something cold to drink. Not a usual beer drinker, he still kept a bottle or two in the refrigerator. Taking one, he returned to the media room and resumed watching.

The sun had tinged the sky when he finally pushed himself up off the sofa. The credits were rolling for the last movie he'd been watching. Squeezing the bridge of his nose, he yawned loudly and stretched. Cal didn't know how many hours he'd been staring at the screen in front of him, but his body was tired.

Taking wobbly steps, he headed for his bedroom. The stunts, which he'd vaguely thought about in the past, awed him now. He understood Piper's reason for returning to the ranch after the investigation. *She* was the prime suspect. The investigation went on for months, and when there was finally a conclusion that found her not responsible for the accident, she disappeared. Cal knew where she'd gone. She'd been truly wrung out by the pressure of the ordeal. He was surprised a film hadn't been made of her experience.

Knowing Piper, she wouldn't agree to such a thing. He also could see why she had her own personal gym on the premises. He figured she used the trick riding in some of the films, but he was unaware of what it took for the dangerous drops, car crashes, jumping off hills and falling off buildings that were involved in her work. The gymnastics equipment was part and parcel of it, of her success. She had to keep in shape if she planned to continue as a stuntwoman, to take the risks she did.

He wondered if she'd made that dangerous decision for her future—and frowned.

"WHEW." NAOMI KNOCKED and opened the door. Her face screwed up and she fanned herself. "You need to shower," she said, not mincing her words.

Cal could say nothing.

"You've been in here going on two days. So you'd better go wash up and let me clean and air out this room."

He stood up, holding his hands out. "Don't clean in here."

"Why not?"

"I still have work to do and I don't want anything moved."

"Ha, that's not going to happen." Naomi gave him her no-nonsense look.

"I'll do it myself," he offered. "When I'm finished with everything."

"You don't have time for that."

"Why not?"

"'Cause that pretty little lady from next door is getting out of her truck right now."

Cal glanced at the window.

"Go," Naomi said, strongly. "I'll try to air the place out."

Cal was already in motion but shouted over his shoulder, "Don't move anything."

Taking the stairs in twos and threes, he pulled his shirt over his head before reaching his room. Hopping on one foot, then the other, he pulled his boots off. His pants and socks followed in quick succession. The bed had not been slept in. He should be sleepy, but he felt energized. In seconds he was under the spray of the shower, hot soapy water beading down his back and over his head.

Five minutes later, Cal was barely dry when he entered the office. He saw immediately that telling Naomi not to clean his office had been the wrong decision. He should have let her do it. Piper stood looking at the papers that were on the desk and those that had fallen on the floor.

"You're investigating me?" she accused. Her voice was low, not a shout and all the more menacing for its low volume.

"It's not like that," Cal tried to explain.

"Then what is it like? All this." She shook the pages in her hands and turned a full circle, encompassing the room. "It's all about me and the accident."

"It is, but—"

"No buts. If you wanted to know something about me, why didn't you just ask? There was no reason to pretend to want lessons and pretend to help me, when your real intention was just—" She stopped.

Cal could only imagine what she intended to say. Whatever it was, it wasn't true.

"Could I get a word in here?" he asked.

Thrusting the pages at him, she pushed them into his chest. "These are all the words you want. They tell you everything. I'm a screwup and it was my fault."

She turned and left, her footsteps angry, her body as straight and hard as stone.

"Piper," he called. She didn't answer or slow down.

He followed her but stopped when the door slammed.

Naomi came up behind him, entering the hallway that led to the front door. "What happened?" she asked.

"I don't know," Cal said.

"Probably had something to do with all those pages and news reports on her accident. I guess she didn't know you were looking into her past. How would you feel if she opened the closet that held your skeletons?"

Naomi drove the dagger further into him. Cal knew what he'd done was wrong. He should have asked her about it, but he thought it would stress her more and she was stressed enough. He should have told her, warned her before she went to wait in his office, yet in retrospect, that was the place they had spent so much time together. Why wouldn't she go there? Especially if she was interested in whether he found out anything more about the accident.

Well, she'd found it. And now he had to backpedal.

"No time like the present to try and smooth things over," Naomi said as if she was his conscience.

"Got any more of that cake?" Cal asked.

JUST AS HE had the first time he approached Piper, he carried two containers of Naomi's cake. He was sure the older woman kept it in the house just to push the two of them together. He headed for Piper's ranch. Cal walked the unpaved path that connected them. The extra time it took to get there would allow him to put his thoughts and emotions in check and hopefully Piper had done the same by then.

He wasn't fighting his attraction to Piper. It was natural. Even though he knew he planned to leave, there was something about her that drew him, forced him to take a closer look at her. He wanted to be around her, protect her, help her prove her innocence. This wasn't totally unlike him. He was often helping someone in one way or another. However, he felt an affinity for Piper. It was stronger with her than he could ever remember feeling before.

Cal tried to fend off the unaccustomed emotions and regain his usual composure. But Piper was on his mind. Somehow he needed her as much as he thought she needed him, even if she didn't think she did. He was compelled to be there for her.

After Piper's stunt was over, after she found her answer, then he could go. And she could return to Hollywood or decide what she'd do next.

Cal stopped at the bottom of the steps and looked up at Piper's front door. He took a deep breath, went up the steps and knocked on the door. Nothing.

He regretted looking into her life without telling her. They had reached a plateau where they were on friendly terms, working together—kissed even—but he'd destroyed that small space he'd hoped would get wider. No chance of that now.

Cal knocked on the door again. He'd hoped, but didn't expect her to answer. When there was no response, he tried the knob. It turned and he walked inside, closing the door loudly enough for her to hear.

"Piper, please, I want to talk to you," he called.

She appeared in the entryway, facing him, her arms crossed in front of her. "What could you possibly have to say? How much you're sorry you invaded my life? How you planned to tell me? How in order to help figure out the accident, you needed all that background information about me? And how I was really at fault? Did I get it all or is there more?"

He walked toward her. Neither Piper nor her folded arms moved.

"You got it all," he said. "Now—" he lowered his voice "—I apologize. I shouldn't have invaded your life without letting you know. I planned to tell you what I found. Yes, I needed background information, but I went further than I should have. I'm a thorough kind of guy, so when I start down a road, I take all the detours to see what the stumbling blocks are. And ultimately, I don't think you were at fault."

Her arms fell to her sides and she stared at him. "You don't?" Her voice was low as if her throat had closed.

Cal shook his head, allowing a smile to creep across his features. Soon, he saw the beginning of her smile. Then she ran across the room and jumped into his arms.

Cal stumbled back a step as her body threw him off balance. The cake containers plopped to the floor. He hugged her back.

"You're the first person who didn't know me before the accident to say that."

He would have gone on holding her, but she pushed herself away.

"Did you find something to support that theory?" she asked. Her voice was slightly higher than normal. He could tell she wasn't totally immune to having feelings for him. Her face had turned a deeper shade of red and her gaze wasn't meeting his.

"Support what?" He was having a hard time concentrating. She had just flown into his arms.

"A problem that caused the failure."

"Oh." Cal finally remembered what they

were discussing. "I could find no flaw in the mechanics. You set up everything perfectly. If anything, it had to be human error, meaning whoever was doing the stunt."

"Austin, the stuntman who was injured, is a professional. He'd done stunts for years. That doesn't mean a veteran can't make a mistake. But I never found anything to indicate he did anything wrong. Did you?"

Cal shook his head.

"Then it had to be me, a flaw in my design," she stated.

"Not necessarily."

Piper's eyes were all but questioning him, imploring him to go on.

"I thought of something we could do," he said.

She raised her brows, again remaining quiet and waiting for whatever his plan could be.

"I have enough information to do a model of the stunt."

"Do you think that would help?" Piper asked.

"No," he said.

"No? Then why—" She spread her hands in confusion.

"I think we should skip the model and go for the real thing. Build it," Cal told her.

"To the exact size and dimensions?" Her eyes widened. Then she blinked several times.

He had to believe she thought he'd taken leave of his senses. He had a fair idea of the monumental task he was proposing, but there were aspects he hadn't encountered before. Yet Cal knew he could work them out.

"Of course," he responded. "Why not? You've got the space for it." Cal spread his arms toward the windows, encompassing the entire ranch. "And you're far enough from town that the zoning laws don't apply to you. Re-creating the problem is the only way to determine what really happened."

"How could we even begin such a venture? We have no equipment, no crew. It takes a massive effort to re-create that framework, not to mention the scores of people needed to pull off the stunt."

Cal kept himself from smiling. Despite her words, she was buying into it. He could tell.

"I've got some ideas on getting a crew."

"Mind sharing them?" she asked.

Cal was excited about this engineering project. His brain practically begged for her to agree. Besides a new build, it would mean spending more time with her.

"There are schools in this part of the world that focus on acting or aspects of filmmaking."

"Perfect," she said. "I've worked with a few of their directors, even did a lecture series for one of them. Depending on how they feel about me and my current circumstances, I might find someone who's willing to help."

"Especially if we can convince the school that this falls under the heading of practical experience."

"Good angle," Piper said. "Not sure if I have any friends left over there, but I'll see."

Her voice was full of optimism, but Cal heard the underlying fear as well. He wondered how long it would be before she started to believe in herself again. She put on a good show and probably most people wouldn't see through to the vulnerability that lay beneath the surface. But he did.

Cal knew it was a risk. Normally, he'd go for the model, but it didn't seem practical. The stunt needed to be re-created, and a model couldn't do that. Nothing short of the real thing would work. And he was sure nothing else would satisfy the Piper he'd come to know in such a short period of time.

THE CAKE SURVIVED the fall. Piper made coffee and they ate it on her porch, looking out on the land where Cal thought the structure could be built.

She finished the dessert and set the empty plate on a small table. Leaning back, she stared at the mountains that seemed so close but were so far away. She knew she was going to have to leave for a lesson soon, but she wanted a moment to just think. Her thoughts weren't on the task before them, but on the past.

"You were researching me," she began.

"I apologi—"

She quickly interrupted him. "His name is Xavier. No doubt you've read that in the research you did."

Cal nodded, saying nothing.

"He's a stunt coordinator with a very lucrative business. Studios pay top dollar for his services."

"You worked there?" Cal asked.

Piper nodded. "I worked for three companies, moving up each time I changed. When I went to work for Xavier, I had specific goals for advancement."

"Did he know that?"

"I laid everything out, down to charts, graphs and costs. He said he was impressed and hired me on the spot."

Cal smiled but still remained quiet.

"Don't you need a script before you decide on the stunts?"

"You do. So I wrote one. At least I wrote a treatment, a story idea. It was rough, but it served to demonstrate the stunts I was using for the presentation."

"The interview?"

"Same thing," she said flippantly.

"How long ago was that?"

"Four years. Even though he hired me, it took a while for me to get my own project." She paused, remembering that day and how thrilled she was that some of her future stunts might be filmed. If only she'd known the disaster that was waiting for her, would she have been able to prevent it? She'd never know.

"And the stunt?" Cal prompted.

"The account in the papers was true. The stuntman overshot the drop point. He had a head injury and three broken bones, two legs and an arm. He was critical for weeks, but he finally pulled through. Unfortunately, he had no memory of the accident."

"So all that was left was you," Cal stated.

"All that was left was me. I had to have made a mistake."

"You weren't the only person working on that stunt."

"But I was in charge. It doesn't matter that I'm not an engineer or a technician. I was responsible for everything about it. Therefore, I was wrong."

"And I see Xavier made sure everyone knew that. From what I read, his comments were very strongly worded."

Piper didn't want to review that part of it. She could still hear her ex's tone and the way he spoke before the review board and the police investigators. Piper was lucky to not have been charged with anything, but her credibility and reputation in Tinseltown were gone with the proverbial wind.

"Stunt work seems very dangerous and a

little unusual for a career choice," Cal said. "How did you get into that?"

"By opening my big mouth at the wrong time."

Cal smiled. "It's a very pretty mouth."

Piper blushed. Heat started at her neck, burned her ears and flooded into her face. Why did Cal have the power to set her off as if she were a human firecracker? No one had ever done that before.

"So, what's the story?" he asked.

Piper looked around at the ranch. "I started right here," she said. "My uncle taught me to ride. One day he saw me fooling around on a horse trying various jumps and tricks I'd seen done on television westerns." She glanced at Cal.

"What happened?"

She nodded. "I got such a stern dressing-down from my uncle that I never did that again." She tried not to laugh but couldn't hold it in. Eventually, it broke through. Cal also laughed. She liked the combination of their voices as they rose into the bright sky.

"I was trying to hit the ground and get back in the saddle while the horse was running. I fell."

Cal raised his brows. "I didn't fall."

"You were lucky. I fell multiple times. After my uncle gave me a thorough tongue-lashing, he woke me up one morning at dawn and took me to the horse barn, where he taught me my first riding trick."

"I bet you were a model student."

"Of course I was." She threw her head back, displaying her mocked indignity. "I was really motivated. I loved doing it, and by the time I was in high school, I was competing."

"You weren't competing. You were winning," Cal corrected. "I've seen your trophy room. Very impressive."

"Thank you. Anyway, while I was at UCLA, I got a summer job at one of the studios. My title was something nice," she smirked. Nice meant terrible. "But my real job was being a glorified gopher. I had to get coffee, get water, get wardrobe. I was always running back and forth. But it was summer and the money was pretty good." She hunched her shoulders, brushing it off. "And here's where the big mouth comes into play."

"I was wondering when you'd get to that."

Again, Cal smiled. And again, Piper's heart flipped.

"There was a horse riding stunt that a stand-in was doing and she kept missing the mark. During a break to reset the scene, I said I could do that better than she could. I didn't know she was standing behind me."

"And she challenged you," Cal finished.

"Loudly. Her voice reached everyone in the company. I had no choice but to accept. So I got on the horse and performed the stunt."

"Flawlessly, I'm sure," Cal said.

"I don't know about that, but I was offered a job as a stunt rider on the spot."

"What did the other rider have to say?"

"She was so angry. Much like Shelby Chase. Venom spewed from her mouth. When she finished with me, she started in on the rest of the crew."

Piper tried to make the memory vanish. She hated scenes that weren't strictly for film.

"Sounds pretty brutal. But…" Cal prompted. "I mean, what happened after that?"

"It backfired on her. The more action work they asked me to do, the more confidence I had in myself, and some of the stunts were elevated. The box office receipts went up and I was called on to do more and more projects. In the end, no one would hire the other woman and she eventually left Hollywood. The last I heard of her, she'd returned to her home in the Midwest and was working at her family's rental car company. And that's how I got into the business."

"Like it?"

"I loved it." She smiled.

"You'll be fine," Cal said.

"You don't know that."

"I do," he said confidently. "You're a winner and you didn't do what they said."

She knew he meant all those who'd believed she'd miscalculated something in the stunt's design. Cal's tone had a softness to it and the underlying conviction made her believe he was right.

She did nothing wrong. Piper knew that in her heart, but she couldn't prove it. At least not yet.

A SOUND WOKE CAL. He groaned, groping for the insistent trill without opening his eyes. It couldn't be morning already, he thought.

He hadn't gone to bed until after two. Opening one eye, he grabbed the clock that had traveled the world with him and shut it off.

The fact that it was dark and the sound continued penetrated his brain. Pushing himself up, he stared at the clock in his hand. It wasn't the alarm clock, but an incoming call. Grabbing the phone, Cal smiled as he pressed the accept button.

"Don't you remember I'm in Montana, where it's two hours earlier than it is in New York and I don't have to be awake at the crack of dawn?"

His brother Jake laughed. "And good morning to you, too. Sorry about the time difference. You were always an early riser. I thought you'd be up by now," his brother said.

"It's different out here, clean air, lots of sunshine, horses to ride every day."

"Are you riding?"

"Every day," Cal yawned. "I'm even taking trick riding lessons."

Jake's laugh was full and loud. "There's got to be a catch to that," he said. "I'm the extreme sports one. At least I was."

Jake had been very athletic, doing thrill

sports, taking dangerous chances. Then he'd been involved in an attack in Paris that had nothing to do with sports. It put him out of commission for a few years. But it was meeting and falling in love with Lauren that changed him. She never asked him to stop doing what he loved. In fact, she encouraged him to do what made him happy. However, Jake said she made him happiest, and after that, they were never far from each other.

Cal envied him. His brother was content, settled in the best possible sense.

"I find the riding fun and the tricks are… let's say entertaining."

Jake laughed again. "Does that mean you spend more time on the ground than in the saddle?"

"Exactly," Cal replied.

"This is something I need to see." Jake's laugh was pure joy.

"Hey, why don't you and Lauren come out? I know two doctors have to have schedules that are hard to change, but—"

"Stop," Jake interrupted. "That's the reason I'm calling. We're attending a medical conference in Seattle next week."

"That's practically in my backyard," Cal

said. They had to get together. He hadn't seen his brother in a year. He'd be willing to fly to Seattle to spend time with him.

"Give or take a state or two or three," Jake joked. "On the way back, we thought we'd stop in Montana and see you."

"Great." This was even better than Cal flying to the coast. Jake and Lauren could stay with him, see the ranch and catch up. "I'll tell Naomi."

"Naomi?"

"She's my housekeeper, although she thinks she's more than that. And she is. Anyway, you'll love her."

"Is she the one giving the trick riding lessons?"

Cal chuckled. "Wait till you meet Naomi. She's a true character."

"Next week," Jake said. "I'll text you the dates."

"Sounds good."

He hung up. Shifting his feet to the floor, he stood. He could never go back to sleep once he was awake. And now he had something to look forward to. After Jake's accident, Cal thought the two of them might be straining their brotherly relationship, but they were closer now than they'd ever been. When Jake and Lauren visited, maybe the four of them could... Cal stopped. Four? He was including Piper in his plans. Usually, it was just his brother and himself getting together and catching up. Now there was Lauren. She didn't know anyone in Montana and they shouldn't leave her with only Naomi for company. Had Cal just assumed he'd bring Piper along? Would she go if he invited her?

He could ask her. She already knew Jake, at least, she knew his reputation. And it would give Cal another chance to spend some time with her.

He liked the thought of that. Sure, they were working together, but *getting* together wasn't part of either's plan. Plans, he thought with a sly smile. Weren't they made to be changed?

CLUTCHING THE LEATHER tether in her hand, Piper led one of Cal's horses in circles. Britt, one of her better students, was in the saddle.

"Sit up, Britt," she said. "Keep your back straight." Usually, she wouldn't use a tether with Britt when riding, but her horse appeared a little jumpy today. Piper thought she'd play it safe. And Britt wasn't her usual self, either.

The young girl did as she was told. She was an excellent rider. But today her attitude seemed different. They went through several exercises and routines. She did them expertly, technically, but with no feeling.

"What's wrong, Britt?"

"Nothing," the young girl said.

"That's obviously not the truth," Piper said. "Why don't you get down and we'll talk. Your lesson is over for today anyway."

Britt climbed down. She was ten years old with long black hair, almost the same color as the horse she preferred. As usual, her students would tie their horses to the post near the fence when done. Britt did the same thing.

"Now, what's bothering you? Your riding was fine, you did everything correct, but your heart wasn't in it."

Britt stroked the mare, running her hand down its nose and along its jawline.

"I wanna learn how to do tricks."

"What?"

"I saw you doing the tricks and I wanna learn that."

Piper leaned against the fence. "Did you see who my student was?" she asked.

Britt nodded. "He owns the Christensen ranch."

"That's right. And he's a little older than you."

"But I can ride," Britt challenged.

"I know and you are excellent at it, but for the moment you're too young."

"What if I get older?"

Piper wanted to laugh, but she'd worked with enough young people to know and understand that to them everything in their lives was of supreme importance.

"When you're a little older, we'll talk about it. And—" The words stopped the joy that seemed to be about to burst on Britt's face. "We'll have to discuss this with your parents."

Her face didn't fall, but it was drawn a bit.

"How old do I have to be?"

"Probably in your teens."

"That long?" she whined.

"Trick riding is dangerous," Piper told her. "If you master your current riding program and you're ready for those lessons when you're fourteen or fifteen, we'll talk to your parents."

"Okay," she said, dragging out the word. Then she quickly looked up. "How about this?" she asked. "How about I come and watch you teaching Mr. Masters?"

"How about I have him come and watch you?"

She frowned, shaking her head.

"Same for him. He doesn't want people watching him, either."

"Okay," she said again, understanding reflected in her eyes.

Britt's mom arrived, and with a wave, the girl was off and running.

Piper smiled and waved as mother and daughter headed home. She supposed word of her giving Cal lessons was out. If Britt knew about them, the other students did, too, along with their parents and probably every other person in Waymon Valley. Piper realized she'd just promised a child that she'd be at the ranch in four or five years when she became a teenager. Was that some kind of premonition? Where would Cal be in five years?

And why did she care?

He seemed to pop into her mind at any time. He was due for a lesson soon. She needed to get ready for that. She couldn't believe how fast he could change directions—change her direction. Piper thought back to their conversation of a few days ago after she'd discovered him looking into her past.

One moment she was so angry with him and the next they were collaborating on re-creating the circumstances surrounding the accident. This time she wanted a different outcome, but discovering the true reason for the tangled metal scaffolding that resulted from a two-minute sequence was the real reason she'd gone along with Cal's plan.

It made sense, Piper thought. She should have thought of it herself. Re-creating the stunt would show her what happened—where the flaw took place.

She didn't have time to think more on that. Cal's truck pulled into the driveway. It was time for his lesson. Piper shook her head, getting rid of her thoughts, and quickly went into the lesson.

Cal did everything she asked of him, and to his credit, he spent less time falling off the horse and getting up from the ground. He was a good student. Like Britt.

"That's it," Piper said when they finished.

Cal jumped down from the horse and grabbed the reins. "Am I going to keep doing the same exercises over and over?"

"Don't be in such a hurry," she cautioned. "When I feel you've mastered the current skill set and you're ready, we'll go on." She gave him a long look that defied him to challenge her.

While Cal didn't seem pleased, he also didn't argue with her. After a minute, he shrugged. "Well, since we can't move on here, maybe we should move ahead with your project."

She nodded. It was what she wanted. Even though she'd been reviewing the accident for over a year, Cal gave her a new perspective and she was more excited about it now than she had been before.

They headed to the house, where she'd set up a workplace. Her small office proved too small for what they needed. They'd commandeered the dining room, which now looked more like a war room with the equipment Cal had brought. His computer, two more monitors, a printer, paper and files. He'd converted the details Tamara had sent into schematics and blueprints. There was a landline telephone that had been at the ranch since she was a child. It was black and heavy and usually sat on a small table near the stairs. Piper plugged it in and set it on the table alongside both their cell phones.

Her cell rang and she saw Tamara's name on the small screen.

"Hi, Tamara," she greeted her. Cal glanced up from the notes he was making. "What's up?"

"Tell me what I hear is not true," Tamara said without the standard greeting.

"What have you heard?"

"That you're planning a do-over of the accident."

"Wow, that was fast. Where did you hear that?" Piper glanced at Cal.

"Does it matter?" she asked. "Is it true?"

"Uh, I'm not re-creating an accident." Piper didn't have to ask which accident. While stunt workers had many unexpected incidents, there was only one that mattered to the two of them. Piper couldn't believe that word of her project had reached California already. Hitting the speaker button, she laid the phone down. "Tamara, Caleb Masters is here with me. He's the engineer on the project. You're on speaker."

She glanced at Cal, who'd stopped what he was doing and looked at the phone.

"So it's true?" Tamara repeated.

"It's true that I'm trying to find out what the cause of the accident was," Piper said. "As for staging an accident, there isn't going to be one."

"How can I help? I don't start filming for another month. I can come there and do whatever you need. I know you're desperate for answers. To be honest, so am I."

Cal and Piper looked at each other. Both raised their eyebrows, then smiled. Cal gave her a thumbs-up.

Piper had to curb her enthusiasm when she responded. She swallowed hard and tried to make her voice as calm as possible. "That would be wonderful, but…"

"But what?" Tamara prompted.

"What about Xavier? Won't you have to tell him where you'll be?"

"I won't hide it. He's got my number. If

something comes up, he can call. I'll be a short plane ride away."

"Only if you charter one. We're a hundred miles from the nearest airport and flights don't happen as often here as they do in LA."

"Then I'll charter one," Tamara said.

Again, Piper looked at Cal.

"We don't want to create any problems." Cal spoke for the first time. His voice was deep and husky. "Your work should come first."

"It will," she said without hesitation. "Being there will give me added experience I need."

Piper knew her friend meant when she began her own business, this experience could help. Being involved in this project would increase her already dense knowledge of running a business and Piper valued her help. Cal hunched and lowered his shoulders, not understanding. Piper didn't feel she could include him in Tamara's plans.

"It's up to you," he said, giving Piper the final decision.

"How soon can you get here?" Piper asked.

"I'll be there tomorrow," she said.

Piper could hear the smile in Tamara's voice.

"Even if chartering my own plane is the only way." Tamara began laughing as if she was finding the humor in her own joke. "I'd like to see the look on Xavier's face when he finds out."

Piper didn't see that as funny. "See you then." She pressed the button ending the call and looked at Cal.

"Nice. You have your first crew member," he said.

"I wonder how she found out about this. Meghan and you are the only people I talked to."

"There's Naomi, who knows everyone in town, and the employees that help run this ranch," Cal said.

"None of them know Tamara."

Piper didn't think to ask Tamara later on how she found out about their plan. She also didn't arrive the next day, but two days later, and by that time the trucks and crews that Cal had called sailed in like an invading armada. He'd cashed in a few favors and Piper had contacted several of the film schools in the area. Since it was summer, she didn't expect much help, but with social media, her phone rang constantly with people asking if she still needed help. She accepted all requests.

Between phone calls and riding lessons, she and Cal continued their nonstop work on the upcoming parameters for the controversial stunt. Piper viewed the table with all its papers and machines. She stood up, weary after what seemed like hours in one position, and stretched. Placing her hands on the small of her back, she bent as far back as she could. Coming to an upright position, she bent forward and grabbed her ankles, then placed her head between her knees.

"Wow," Cal said from his seat at the table. He looked upside down from her position. "I've seen some flexible people, but you don't seem to have joints."

Piper laughed and stood up straight. Her back still hurt. Remembering something she'd do on set, Piper lay down on the floor. She stretched her arms above her head and extended her feet in a taut hold.

"What are you doing?" Cal asked. This time he got up and came around, peering down on her.

"Stretching," she said. "I've been in one spot too long. I should have gotten up and moved, but we were so into the process that I forgot."

That was what he did to her. Thoughts of things that came naturally were totally off-kilter when Cal came anywhere near her. And they were constantly together these days.

Cal spun a chair around and sat in it. With his hands, he flexed his fingers, indicating that she should come to him. Piper sat up and another hand gesture had her turning her back to him. He began massaging her shoulders and back.

Her eyes closed. His fingers spread warmth through her muscles, easing the tension. She could sit there the rest of the day as long as his hands kept moving, drawing circles and spreading heat and relaxation all over her.

"How'd you get to work with a star like Elisabeth Grey?" Cal broke into her thoughts.

"It was an accident," Piper said. "I literally fell into it."

"You what?" Cal asked, sounding amused. "Really?"

Piper's head bobbed up and down.

"What happened?"

Piper was enjoying the massage but tried to concentrate on remembering her first encounter with Elisabeth.

"I was finished for the day, but Elisabeth Grey was working and I wanted to see her. I was trying to be quiet on the set, but I tripped and fell directly into the stunt coordinator's arms." She laughed, recalling the moment. "I disrupted the entire scene."

"But you got hired?"

"No, I got fired."

"That seems like a mistake on their part," Cal said.

"I thought so, but my credentials weren't revoked immediately. I still wanted to see Elisabeth Grey. So, I went back to the set and watched. It was an outside scene, so no one noticed an extra person standing around, especially since I was known by some of the crew. Elisabeth did her bit and then her double stepped in, but the stunt didn't go as planned. She missed her timing and fell behind the horse she was supposed to ride." Piper stopped thinking of her own upcoming stunt. "No one was hurt." She rushed to explain.

"So it was actually a second stunt exhibition that got you a job with a global star?"

"That and my excellent sense of timing," she teased. "But it wasn't all glory."

"What did you do?"

"I said I could do the stunt. I really shouldn't have pushed my way in, but they were at a loss, and the longer they waited to sort out a solution, the more money it was costing the studio."

"Wow, that's either a wild or a brave thing to do," Cal stated.

"Exactly. Without thinking or asking anyone, I started running. There was a ramp. I hit it and flipped head over heels into the air and came down on a platform. From there, I mounted a horse from the rear and began riding. I did a few other things I knew Elisabeth would do, but they weren't in the script. When I got to the fence, I was supposed to go around. I jumped it instead. The horse had a jumper's saddle and I saw no reason to avoid the makeshift fence. Then I slowed the horse and walked it back to the place where I started."

Cal laughed. In hindsight, she knew she

was showing off, but her uncle had taught her well and the horse was a jumper.

"What happened then?"

"I was surrounded. People came from everywhere, all talking at once, most shouting. There were the animal control people, who said I had no right to do the stunt. I tried to tell them I'd grown up with horses and would never, ever hurt one. But my voice was lost in all the hoopla. Other people were shouting questions, asking how I could do that, where had I learned it, all sorts of things. They came too fast for me to answer any of them."

"Were you officially fired after that?"

"Not exactly. I was fired by the stunt company I worked for and stripped of access to the set."

"But…" Cal prompted.

"Before the day ended, I got a full-time job doing stunts with the company working on the Elisabeth Grey movie."

"Doing Elisabeth Grey's stunts?"

Piper nodded. "She was the defining voice. She went to bat for me, saying she wanted me to do her stunt work and be her stand-in."

"Even though you'd never worked with her before?"

"Even though. But she's a cool person, and when the opportunity came out of the blue like that, I went for it."

Cal stared at her for a long moment. Piper looked up and knew it was hard for him to comprehend. He operated in a finite world. She worked in one that was more fluid. Scripts could change from one minute to another. Actors—and chances—came and went. Accidents happened. Any number of delays or starts and stops could occur.

"Why don't we take a break?" Piper suggested.

Cal nodded.

"I'll get us something to drink and bring it to the porch." The air was refreshing when she stepped through the door a few minutes later. Setting a tray on the small table, Piper poured them iced tea and took a seat. Her muscles felt a lot better, especially since she'd taken time in the kitchen to stretch again.

Cal drank from his glass, looking out over the vista of grass. He was quiet so long that she wondered what he was thinking.

"Do you miss California?" he asked after several minutes of silence.

Turning her head, she looked at him. His face was serious.

"Sometimes," she said.

She smiled, but it wasn't totally a happy smile, yet it wasn't sad, either. "Being in movies, whether acting or any area for that matter, is hard work. The actors make it look easy and there's an entire crew of people making it look flawless for the public, but there is a lot of money, sweat and tears that go into making a movie."

"Isn't there just as much work doing stunts as there is acting?"

"Absolutely. And the danger is much greater, but the reward is tenfold." She paused as past memories flooded her mind.

"But what about that danger? The stunts are a real risk and must involve a lot of work."

"The danger is real. It is," Piper said. "But there are good people I've worked with, professionals committed to their trade. And I don't have to be the person climbing the scaffolding or jumping off the plane all the time. There are plenty of talented stunt people for the screen. And more and more computer-generated images are used. The industry is changing with the technology. I just have to keep up with it."

"The actors do also, don't they?"

"Not as much. There are some who love technology, but most just want to develop the character they are playing."

"From what I observed while we worked on our plan, you love the programming, what the systems can tell you," Cal said.

She smiled. "I do. It's a whole new world out there. And I love being part of it." She looked down. "Only, I'm not."

"You will be," Cal assured her. "Once we get this up and running, the outcome will be different and you'll know what happened."

"You can't be sure of that," she told him. "There may be something we don't know, some variable that doesn't work its way into our calculations. Something that all the papers, photos and notes haven't revealed. Or maybe there's an assumption we make that is wrong."

"There's always an element of the unknown," Cal agreed. "But it's the best chance we have."

"We," she said, her brows rising. She smiled at him. "You're always so positive that the outcome will be exactly what I want it to be. I don't know what I've done to make you have such faith in me."

"Don't you?"

Piper could only stare at Cal. Her legs grew heavy as if she was planted to the ground. Her mouth dropped open and she consciously closed it. What did he mean? Of course, she knew what he meant.

"Cal, we should keep this professional."

"I know," he said. "But it gets harder every day."

THE FOLLOWING DAYS took on a life of their own. Trucks delivering everything, people arriving, Cal and Tamara arranging where to stack supplies and equipment. Piper's mind reeled at the rapidity of 18-wheelers rumbling along the ridge with metal girders and cranes to drop off. A parade of dump trucks followed with everything from screws to sand.

The Hotel Emily was overwhelmed with guests. Tamara was the only one staying with Piper. Naomi appeared in her element with so many folks underfoot. Of course, she corralled them like wayward children. Tamara took control of the overall organization, directing where the vehicles should park and what was unloaded and stored where.

With all the activity, Piper's mind was constantly on Cal. She'd told him they should keep things professional, yet she was the one who wanted to cross the line. She knew better. There would be no turning back for her if she did. And then what would happen to her when he acted on those job offers he had? Her heart was in danger and she knew it. Better to keep as much distance between them as she could. That was a task harder than she anticipated.

Cal came up behind Piper, who was watching all the activity. She steeled herself, hiding the onslaught of emotion that flowed within her every time they came into close proximity.

They didn't touch. Piper made a point of putting space between them. But the heat level in the air rose undeniably. For her, anyway. She wasn't sure Cal felt it. He'd been nothing but professional since their last conversation. It was as if there was a wall around him. She wondered if he was protecting his feelings as she was protecting hers.

"This is really happening." She glanced his way, then back at all the activity.

"Were you in any doubt?" he teased.

Despite the wall, he'd been trying to ease the tension. She wanted to help but didn't know how.

Finally, Piper shrugged. "I didn't picture it this way. Usually when I arrive on a set, all this has been done."

"This time it's your show, start to finish," he said.

"That's a little scary. More than a little. It's terrifying."

"You'll do fine. I've got your back," he said. "And so do all those people."

He slipped his arm around her waist. They were on the other side of the ridge, away from the house and the horse barn. Piper couldn't help the audible intake of breath that his touch produced. It felt natural. She leaned back for a second, wanting to stay in his embrace. But she didn't want to get used to him holding her. Except she did want to get used to it.

And that scared her.

Someone calling her name gave her the excuse to move. Meghan was walking up the hill toward them and apparently leading a brigade of people. Piper recognized a few of them from town. She scanned the faces. She saw Reverend Pyne and assumed most of them were part of the church congregation. He nodded at her, but no one else gave her a clue as to why they were here. Shelby Chase, at the rear of the group, was flanked by at least ten of her students, Piper guessed. Her heart fell. She hoped they weren't here to protest her actions. It *was* her land. And Cal had checked the zoning requirements. She was within the law and her rights.

"Meghan, what's going on?" Piper asked when the crowd stopped in front of her and Cal.

"They're here to help," she said and smiled, glancing over one shoulder and then the other.

"Help?" Piper looked at the group again.

"Let me explain." Ally, the diner owner, stepped forward. "Meghan told us what you're doing." She smiled at Meghan. "We want to help you out. You're working on a shoestring." She gestured to the crowd behind her. "We've all been there. We have car-penters, electricians, all kinds of professions represented, plus, people who are willing to learn. And I'll be supplying the afternoon meal."

"Why?" Piper asked, clearly confused. "I haven't been very friendly to any of you." She looked out over the group.

One person called out, "You're right about that." It caused a round of laughter.

"But you're one of us," Ally said.

Piper frowned, still confused that they would include her.

"Just as your parents are and your aunt and uncle," Meghan said. "They were a large part of Waymon Valley and you are, too."

"I hate to say it," Cal whispered so only she could hear. "But here's a gift horse. Don't look it in the mouth. We could use all the extra hands and brainpower we can get."

Piper smiled. "Thank you." Her voice cracked as emotion welled up inside her. No one had been this welcoming of her since before she left for Hollywood and it was her own fault. She swallowed. "If you're here to help, I won't refuse. And from now on, I'll do better to live up to the values my family taught me."

She heard positive noises pass through the crowd, along with many smiles and a few hands raised in salute.

"Tamara, the woman with the long, dark hair over there giving directions—" she pointed to her friend "—she'll tell you where to put your things and who to work with. After you're all settled, Cal and I will have a meeting at seven tonight to go over what's been done and what still needs doing."

The crowd broke up. Some were nodding. Some were smiling. And of course, some held the stalwart countenance that Montanans were known for. It didn't mean they weren't on board, just that they didn't readily show their feelings.

"I can't thank you enough," Piper repeated. Emotion welled up in her and she could hardly contain it. She felt guilty. They were here for her when she'd been distant and isolated.

As the group moved away, Meghan came forward.

"You did good." She smiled.

"This is all your doing," Piper whispered as if it were a conspiracy.

"Not all. We're a family here. You should remember that."

"You're right. I guess you're thinking of the summer we were fifteen."

"That's one instance."

"What happened?" Cal asked.

Piper turned to him. "There was a major thunderstorm in the middle of the night. Lightning struck the Swanson barn and it burned to the ground."

"The town was a lot smaller back then," Meghan added. "We all pitched in and re-built it."

"And several ranchers helped make up the lost produce," Piper supplied.

"Sounds like a great town," Cal said.

"Exactly," Meghan agreed. "We were in high school then, but we helped with the horses and the farm animals." Meghan laughed again. "You should have seen Piper after she fell in the mud trying to catch a pig. She had mud everywhere and the pig got away."

"That's not funny," Piper said.

Meghan looked at Cal. "She had such a crush on Jeff Swanson."

"We don't need to revisit that, Meghan."

"Sure, she does," Cal said. "I'm intrigued. I'd like to hear more."

"Well, you must know by now that Piper has to prove that she can do anything as well as the next guy."

Cal glanced from one woman to the other. Piper hunched her shoulders and dropped them.

"I was right more times than I was wrong," she said, tossing her hair back.

"Not when you went headfirst into the muck and Jeff watched you fall."

"Only that one time. And, of course, he had to be there to see it."

Meghan gave her a knowing nod and waved goodbye.

Piper and Cal watched Meghan join the crowd Tamara was handling. A cloud seemed to settle over Piper.

Cal took her hands. "It's going to be fine," he said.

Piper looked away. "That's not it," she said.

"What is, then?"

She took a long time to answer. "I feel so guilty. I mean, look at them, coming here to help someone who did little to gain their friendship."

Cal stepped closer to her. Piper had to tilt her head to see his face.

"You have the opportunity to change that." He nodded at the group. "They seem like a great community."

"I know," she said. "They've offered me a chance. It's up to me to take it."

And she would.

CHAPTER EIGHT

A CAR DOOR slammed outside. Cal pushed his chair back, the wheels squeaking as they rolled across the floor in his office. Standing up awkwardly, he started for the hall. He'd been listening for the sound of their car for an hour. His brother and sister-in-law were due. And they were finally here. Cal's stride was longer than normal as he headed to the door. It had been a year since he'd seen Jake, and Cal was looking forward to getting together with him.

The brothers had always been close, except for a small stretch of time after Jake's accident. They were back on track now.

Cal practically jumped down the porch steps. Jake was out of his seat just as Cal's boots hit the ground. Clasping hands, they pulled each other into a warm hug, their grins as wide as their faces.

Lauren came around the car and Cal

pulled her into the hug. "Keeping him in line?" Cal asked as he stood back, glancing at his brother, then at her.

"I'm trying," she said. "But since he got that arm back, he's into everything."

They all laughed, but they knew the reason that caused Jake to lose the use of his right arm was no laughing matter. It had taken two full years and Lauren's unconventional guidance before any feeling came back to his arm.

Fully recovered and married, his brother looked healthy and happy.

"How was the drive?" asked Cal.

Instead of flying from Seattle, they'd chosen to rent a Jeep and drive, using the time as a mini vacation.

"I loved it," both husband and wife said simultaneously. Again, they all laughed. Cal thought of all the times they had laughed together. It was going to be a great weekend. He couldn't wait for them to meet Piper.

Lauren moved around, turning in a full circle to take in the land as far as she could see. Cal had done the same thing the first time he arrived in the Valley.

"It's beautiful," she said. "No wonder you want to stay here."

"I haven't decided that yet," he said. "In fact, I'll probably be leaving for another job soon."

They started up the porch steps.

"Sometimes, I think my wanderlust rubbed off on you," Jake said.

"I think we both have it to a degree."

Jake stopped on the porch. "Where are the horses?" he asked.

"Next door."

Jake looked in all directions. "We live in Manhattan," he said. "Next door is ten feet away if that."

Cal pointed toward Piper's ranch. "It's on that ridge." They all focused on the area where he pointed. Piper's house could be seen in the distance.

"I can't wait to go for a ride," Jake said. "It's been on my mind since I called you."

"Aren't you tired?" Cal asked. "It was a long ride here."

"We took our time, stayed overnight at an inn about a hundred miles from here."

"And we're doctors," Lauren pitched in. "We're used to working long periods of time."

Half an hour later, the brothers raced across the open field. Horse hooves pounded the soft earth. The wind rushed toward them, pressing its spiny fingers against their faces. Neither spoke, but Cal saw the smile on Jake's face as he controlled his horse. It had been years since they were together like this. For Cal, the years fell away like dominoes crashing into one another, clearing the path back to memories of their boyhood escapades.

Pulling up, they slowed to a stop. Cal affectionately patted the horse's neck, letting it know he was proud of its performance.

"Wow, I missed this," Jake said, his voice a little winded.

"Me, too. You and Lauren don't ride?"

He looked around at the open space. "Not like this," he said. "There's nothing here but air and sky as far as you can see. I could ride for days, go as fast as the horse would let me and not worry about anything except me and the wind."

Cal gazed about. The openness was one of the things that he liked about Montana. The mountains to the west were far in the distance. Huge hills banked the east, shielding the valley.

"I know what you mean. I ride like that sometimes." Cal suddenly laughed. "Remember when we used to ride like this on the beach near Granny's house?"

Jake threw his head back and let out a belly laugh. "Then she'd come running and scold us for it."

"She was right. Remember some of the foolish things we did that she never knew about?" Cal said.

Again, both brothers chuckled.

"Speaking of foolish things, I want to see some of the tricks you've learned," Jake said.

Cal looked back toward the house. Then he glanced at Piper's ranch. She had a lesson going on and was on the far side of the barn.

"I'm not supposed to do this without the instructor, but this is something I've been practicing."

"Just like you to show off for the teacher," Jake grinned.

Cal scowled at him. "I get it from you."

"Did you forget you're the older brother?"

Cal didn't reply. Curling his fingers around the horse's reins, he kicked his legs and took off. From a canter to a full run, he crossed the plain. Then holding on to the reins and saddle horn, he pulled his weight up, arching his leg over the horse and out of the stirrups. For a moment his boots hit the ground, causing a scattering of dirt. Using the momentum of his legs and the motion of the horse, Cal swung himself back in the saddle.

Pleased with his performance, he let out the breath he was holding and slowed the animal to a walk, returning to where his brother waited. He stopped alongside Jake.

And that was when he saw her.

Cal's heart pounded and he felt the sudden cold fear that accompanies getting caught doing something you're not supposed to.

Jake picked up on his gaze and looked toward the horse and rider bearing down on them with the speed of lightning.

"I take it that's your trainer," he said. "From the look of fury, you'd better be prepared for one of those Granny scoldings."

"That's her." Cal knew this was going to be worse than anything his granny ever did.

Piper's red hair flared out behind her. She wore neither hat nor helmet. Cal was sure she'd just jumped on her horse when she saw what he was doing and hightailed it up the ridge.

"Have you forgotten what I'd told you?" she said, pulling up next to Cal. She grabbed the reins of his horse and yanked them out of his hands. "You could have killed yourself. Not to mention harmed this animal."

"But I didn't do either of those things. I got it right."

"Lucky for you." Her voice was guttural and gritty. Her breath hard and audible. "This is not a trained horse. It's got the wrong saddle and you're not an experienced enough rider yet."

She glanced at Jake, her eyes piercing, yet she said nothing to him. Returning her attention to Cal, she said, "You've exercised him enough. Take him back to the barn and cool him down. And do it at a walk."

Cal felt just like he did when his grandmother reprimanded him. "I'm sorry," he said. "I was showing off for my brother." He raised a brow at Jake, who gave him no help.

"Hello, Doctor," she addressed him. "Sorry we're meeting under these circumstances." Again, with her features stern, she reprimanded Cal.

Jake frowned. "Have we met?"

She shook her head. "I've only seen pictures of you and read articles."

Jake looked surprised. He glanced at Cal.

"I used to work in Hollywood. One of the producers wanted to make a movie about your life, but you refused."

"I remember that. Small world," Jake said. "And Cal didn't mean to do anything wrong. He was showing me what he'd learned. At my request," he added.

She focused on Cal. "He knows better. You should get the horses back."

Nodding at Jake, she galloped back toward her barn.

"You didn't say you were taking lessons from a woman as beautiful and headstrong as they come," Jake accused.

"She is that," Cal agreed. Beautiful and headstrong described her perfectly.

Jake chuckled. "Be careful, the last beautiful, headstrong woman I met, I married."

PIPER WAS STILL angry with Cal when he arrived for his lesson the next morning.

"I said I was sorry. What more can I do?" Cal followed Piper out of the barn. She led the horses they were to ride for his lesson. She was too annoyed with him to speak. "Haven't you ever made a mistake during training?"

She stopped so suddenly, he walked into her. Cal saw her begin to turn. It was like watching a movie where the character turns so slowly, the audience knows something terrible is about to happen. When she finally faced him, her eyes blazed hot enough to melt steel.

"I didn't mean that," he apologized again, realizing that he'd crossed the line. Her being in Montana had everything to do with a mistake. Yet his words appeared to get through to her. Piper sighed and her shoulders relaxed. She took a couple of steps back.

"I realize you wanted to show your brother what you've learned, but please don't do it again."

Cal raised both hands defensively, palms out. "I promise," he said.

"Unless…" She paused. "Unless I'm there with you. And you only do what I tell you to do."

"I promise," Cal said. "It wasn't my intention to hurt the horse and I had learned…"

Piper stopped him with a gesture. "You've had a few lessons. You can ride, but you are not ready for performing trick moves alone. You could have hurt yourself, the horse and my reputation."

Cal hadn't thought of that. Did he hear concern in her voice for him or for the horse? Giving himself a mental shake, he decided she was more concerned about the horse than about him. And she should be. His act had been thoughtless. Her reputation was on the line, and for all he knew, riding lessons could be her only source of income. He didn't want to damage that.

He also didn't want her upset with him.

"I apologize again. I didn't think of all the ramifications I could cause you. I should have. It's my business to be responsible for an entire job. I should have thought that you were in the same boat."

"Apology accepted," Piper said.

Cal blew out a breath. "Now that you're no longer angry with me, I've made reservations for dinner tonight at the Emily. Would you like to join us?"

"No," she said quickly and succinctly.

Piper started walking. Cal noticed that

whenever she didn't want to deal with a situation, she took off. He followed her.

"And don't give me that line about I have to eat. I can eat when I want to and where I want to."

"So what's wrong with the Emily at seven o'clock?" he asked.

"Nothing—"

"Good. I'll pick you up at six thirty."

"I didn't say I'd go and stop trying to push me. I can make my own decisions."

"I wasn't questioning that," Cal said. "I enjoy your company and thought you'd like a night out."

"You mean a date," she said.

"If you want to call it that?"

"What else would I call it?"

"Dinner with friends. I am a friend." He lowered his voice to both a seductive and understanding nature. "Light conversation, no judgment, relaxed atmosphere and meeting a couple of new people. My brother and his wife will be there." Cal smiled encouragingly. "Say you'll go."

She hesitated for some time. Cal held his breath. He really wanted her to go with him. Even if Jake and Lauren hadn't been visiting, he'd still want to spend time with her. And not just when he was taking his lessons.

"You make it so hard to say no," she said. "I really would like to meet your brother. And his wife." She frowned. "I mean when I'm not scathingly ticked off with you," she said.

Cal heard her smile even if it wasn't on her lips.

"Fine. It will give me a chance to try and make up for the first impression I gave him."

"Six thirty sharp," he said.

THE EMILY'S FORMAL dining area was as different from the smaller gold and white room where Piper and Meghan had eaten lunch weeks earlier, as a sandwich shop was from a White House state dinner. That day felt like a lifetime ago now that she was here with Cal and his family. Outfitted with white tablecloths and fancy chair coverings, it was an elegant space perfect for a special meal or an important occasion. Piper had never seen the room this way before.

Opting for the teal chiffon dress she'd worn to the Oscars two years ago was the right decision. She fluffed her skirt and switched her matching bag from one hand to the other.

"Please come this way," the maître d' said, selecting several large black velvet-covered menus. Cal put his hand on her elbow. His light touch was warm. She felt a tingle where his hand made contact with her bare skin. Tonight, she wasn't sure if he'd forgotten their conversation and his practice of keeping an arm's length between them or if it was just natural to guide her through the room. Either way, she wished the room was miles long instead of the short trip to their table in the center of the room.

Smiling, she took a seat. Cal hovered behind her, helping with her chair, being very attentive. Why she felt like a queen, she didn't know. She hadn't had a feeling like this since she was in high school and the captain of the basketball team asked her to the school dance. Clearly, Cal wanted to impress her. She wondered if he was having any of those thoughts. Did he want to impress her?

The idea caused a strange stirring in her stomach. It wasn't from being hungry. She could feel his nearness. His hand was warm when she sat back and it was still resting on the chair. Piper forced her eyes to remain open when the urge to close them and appreciate his kindness was as strong as ever. She was both relieved and disappointed when he sat in the chair next to her.

"Piper, Caleb tells us you work in the movies in Hollywood," Lauren said when they were seated and had ordered. "That sounds so exciting."

"It is," she said truthfully. Yet she wondered how much of her story Cal had shared.

"Piper is the stunt double for Elisabeth Grey," Cal relayed.

Piper saw both Jake's and Lauren's brows rise. "Really?" Jake said. "I never thought I'd like action movies, but hers I do enjoy. Now that I know you're the person doing all that running, jumping and falling, I'll appreciate watching them even more."

Piper smiled. "Was," she said. "I *was* Elisabeth's double. My friend Tamara St. John does her stunt work now."

"Did you ever get hurt?" Jake asked. "Some of those leaps and falls look so real."

"I haven't in the past," she said. "But accidents do happen." She left it at that.

Piper didn't want to talk about herself. People looked at Hollywood as some magical playland. In truth, it was hard work and could be an unforgiving place. The finished product made it seem easy, but Piper knew better. She also knew she didn't want to fall into a discussion that led back to *the* accident, as she knew it inevitably would.

Taking control of the discussion, Piper shifted the focus to Jake. "A few years ago, I might have been working on a film involving you, Dr. Masters, as I mentioned the other day."

The water glass Lauren was holding stopped halfway to her mouth as she looked at her husband. "You never told me that," she said.

"I was approached, but I refused," Jake said. "It was over and done with in a moment."

Piper knew that was an exaggeration. When a producer got his or her hooks in a story, refusal by the subject usually made them bear down harder. She knew Jake Masters had refused to see them or take their calls.

"Before or after you met me?" Lauren asked.

"After, if you include the fact that we met in college," he told her. "But before you pretended to be my companion."

"Companion? Pretended?" Piper seized on the words. "That's intriguing." She looked from face to face for an explanation.

Lauren smiled at Cal. "It's all Caleb's fault," she said, putting her hand on Jake's.

"While I was attending a medical conference in Paris, there was a terrorist bombing and I was injured," Jake said.

"Critically," Cal added.

Piper nodded. She knew the story.

"After seeing hundreds of doctors to no avail," Jake embellished.

"Caleb hired me to act as Jake's companion," Lauren continued. "I couldn't tell Jake that I was a doctor. Not even that I was a children's doctor. He'd seen too many physicians and he was angry. At all of us."

"I wasn't angry," Jake protested.

She nodded. "All right, he was…contentious."

"Fed up with being probed," Jake explained. "I just wanted to be left alone. But this insistent *companion*—" he stressed the word, taking the sting out with a smile "—wouldn't let me be."

"Good thing, too," Cal said.

"I admit it," Jake said and smiled. "She got under my skin." Their fingers linked.

Piper's eyes went to Cal's fingers. She wasn't sure why. She thought of him brushing his hand against her back when she sat down. She wondered about that special touch between husband and wife and whether she'd ever feel it.

"Go on, Piper. Why did you want to make a movie about Jake?" Lauren asked.

Shaking off her thought, Piper returned her attention to the conversation and the trio of people sitting with her. "It wasn't me. I worked for the stunt company at the time. The producers wanted to make the film and I saw the specs. They wanted to use Jake's passion for extreme sports as a jumping-off point, then add the Paris bombing and his recovery as the plot of the story. When the refusal came and there was no chance of the project getting off the ground, everything was filed away but not forgotten. In years to come, someone may pull it out and try again."

Jake was shaking his head even before she finished speaking. "I'm a doctor. That's all anyone needs to know," he said.

Piper understood. Autobiographies of living people could be embarrassing, especially when the magic factory put a dramatic spin on it. It was clear Jake Masters was aware that pinning his name to a contract opened his life up to scrutiny. Piper knew from experience how devastating that could be.

The waiter arrived with their food and the subject changed to Piper's riding lessons. It was a subject she didn't mind talking about.

"Do you ride?" Piper asked Lauren.

"Not really. I was on a pony when I was about seven. And once while in college, I went riding with some friends. I still remember the muscle pain the next few days produced."

Piper smiled. "Like any exercise, the muscles stop protesting with continued use."

"Oh, it wasn't the horse so much as my repeated contact with the ground that was the problem."

After the laughter died down from her comment, Piper said, "You should come over and ride with me while you're here. I'll make sure you stay on the horse."

"That's a great idea," Cal said.

"I'm not sure of that," Lauren replied with a frown.

"I promise to take it easy on you, so the discomfort—" Piper added air quotes around the word "—won't be too bad."

"All right," Lauren said slowly, skepticism evident in her tone. "Jake likes to ride. If I learn, we could do it together. But we're only going to be here for the weekend. Back in New York, I doubt we'll get the chance for much riding."

Piper noticed a change in Lauren when she mentioned her husband. It was obvious how much in love they were. It wasn't just the way they looked at each other, although the air between them practically spelled out *l-o-v-e* in large visible letters. It was how much in tune with each other they were.

Would anyone ever love her that much? Piper wondered. If her past relationships were a barometer, it wasn't going to happen. Then she looked at Cal, whose eyes were on her. She saw interest in them and quickly looked away.

Her stomach fluttered. Yet she knew Cal wasn't the one. Literally he would go east and she west. They were the twain that would never meet.

CAL RELAXED AS soon as the conversation began at dinner. The evening was pleasant and friendly as he'd hoped it would be. He wanted his brother and sister-in-law to like Piper. She needed friends. And he liked Piper. Liked her a lot. They talked about everything from the movies to medicine, with additional anecdotes on Cal's involvement with certain horses and the trick riding lessons he was taking.

The laughter was frequent and joyful. If Piper felt tense or uncomfortable, she didn't show it. She seemed to get along with both his brother and sister-in-law.

Cal and Jake exchanged a look that told Cal his brother thought his lessons were more about Piper than riding a horse. He wasn't wrong. Cal couldn't put his finger on why, but the feelings were there. Tonight, as she talked to Lauren and Jake, he came to appreciate her even more.

"When we were riding along that ridge," Jake began, "I noticed you're building something huge. Are you expanding your riding school?"

Cal watched Piper, waiting for her face to fall. It didn't, at least not totally. A faint amount of color seeped under her skin, but the restaurant lighting camouflaged it.

"That's a project your engineer brother and I are working on."

"I knew he couldn't stay still for long." He looked at Piper. "He's been telling us that he's just relaxing out here."

"For the most part, that's true," Cal stated.

Again, Cal glanced at her. Her face was unreadable.

"I'm helping Piper work on a stunt."

"Does that mean you're returning to your business in California?" Lauren asked, her voice hopeful.

"Maybe," Piper said. "It depends on the outcome of our project."

"Well, good luck with it," Jake added.

Piper nodded.

The waiter brought them coffee and they lingered over the meal, talking and exchanging stories for a long time. The mood lightened after the brief discussion of the scaffold that was going up in Piper's yard. Cal wished they could have stayed longer. Piper, however, had lessons in the morning. More supplies were expected and Tamara needed help.

They left the restaurant laughing, having spent an enjoyable evening. As they walked to the vehicle, Cal noted Lauren slipping her arm through Jake's and his hugging her close. Cal wanted to do the same to Piper but tactfully kept his arms at his sides.

The drive back was quiet and cordial. Cal stopped in front of his house, where Lauren and Jake got out.

"You're still coming to ride tomorrow, right?" Piper asked Lauren through the window.

"Tomorrow? That soon?" Lauren asked.

Piper smiled and Lauren nodded.

"Remember, I haven't been on a horse in decades."

"Not a problem," Piper assured her.

"No tricks," Lauren warned.

"Not a single one."

With that, Piper threw a look at Cal. The

story of his ride and Piper's hot reaction had played out more than once since it happened.

Husband and wife stepped away from the truck.

"I'll be right back," Cal said, reversing the vehicle and heading down the driveway.

"No hurry," Jake said. "Take *all* the time you need."

JAKE'S ENCOURAGING WORDS weren't lost on Piper. She both heard and understood his tone. The atmosphere in the cab changed when she and Cal were alone. The darkness seemed heavier. The distance between them more intimate, as if somehow the interior had shrunk and they were closer together. It took less than ten minutes to reach her house by the road, yet she felt the drive was nearly as long as the country was wide.

Taking a deep breath and corralling her emotions, she was in control when Cal parked and opened the door for her.

"Thank you for asking me to go tonight," Piper said as she slipped down from the passenger side of the truck. Cal closed the door.

"I was glad you came," he said.

"I enjoyed myself. I'd forgotten how much fun it is to share a meal with and talk to new people."

She was sure he resisted saying I told you so.

"We should do it more often," Cal suggested.

She didn't respond. They walked toward the steps leading to her porch. She had genuinely had a good time tonight. Cal's family was delightful. The stories they told and all the laughter was more therapeutic than any other remedy. Meeting Jake and Lauren and interacting with them showed Piper how starved she'd been for friendship. And Cal being there only made the night complete.

A wave of guilt struck her as she remembered the town coming to her rescue. She hadn't changed her mind about being more active with them, either. And being more friendly.

They reached the porch steps.

"What time are you and Lauren going riding?" Cal asked.

"Right after your lesson. Tamara can handle things here. And don't ask to go with us. It's strictly a ladies-only affair."

"That sounds ominous."

"They'll only be here for the weekend," Piper said. "Her riding with me will give you and your brother time to catch up and bond."

"I'm sorry they can't stay longer. It had been a while since we spent any time together," Cal said.

"Since they're both doctors, I imagine they have very busy schedules."

"They do. When I was away on jobs, we might not see each other for a long time. Thankfully, these last few months have meant less traveling for me."

Piper stepped up on the first step. Cal stayed on the walkway.

"That was very nice of you," he told her.

"What?"

"Asking Lauren to ride with you."

Piper smiled. "I like her. We'll probably talk more than ride."

Cal stiffened. "Talk? About what?"

"What women always talk about when they get together—men." The corners of her mouth turned up.

"Men in general or someone specific?"

"What's the fun in being general when there are two of you close at hand?"

CHAPTER NINE

THE WEEKEND FLEW by faster than Piper thought time could move. She and Lauren spent hours in the saddle, but mostly they shared a lot of laughter while appreciating Naomi's meals. At night the four of them went dancing or relaxed under the galaxy of overhead stars. Piper truly liked both Lauren and Jake. She looked forward to spending time with them each day when her lessons were done. Cal and his brother seemed to solidify the inseparable bond that was already there.

Piper didn't have that kind of relationship with her sibling. There was little animosity between them, but the kind of sharing Cal had with his brother was different from anything she had with her brother. Their lives were too different, their interests too diverse and the physical distance between them contributed to their lack of family togetherness.

Even though she didn't know it was missing from her life, she longed for it now.

Finally, real life intervened and the fun weekend came to an end. By the time Lauren and Jake waved goodbye, half of the structure to re-create the accident was built and it was back to work full-time. On Monday morning, Piper stepped out on her porch and surveyed the area. She didn't have any lessons coming up, and with Jake and Lauren gone, she felt a little lonely.

Tamara joined her, a cup of coffee in her hands. "Didn't see much of you this weekend. So how was your time with the Family Masters?"

"Don't be dramatic," Piper said lightly, although she could feel the color rising in her face. She turned toward the ridge and looked out over the horizon away from Cal's ranch.

"I know you like him," Tamara stated.

"Of course I do. I don't usually work with people I don't like."

Both of them knew that wasn't the whole truth.

"Well," Tamara said, perched on the railing and balancing her weight against the post. One leg swung back and forth. "There is like and then there's *like*."

"Don't get any ideas. Spending the weekend with nice people doesn't mean I'm joining the family."

"Do you want to?" Tamara asked.

Piper gave Tamara a scathing look, and for a moment, she couldn't speak. She swallowed hard. "I think it's time we went back to work. I feel like I abandoned you this past weekend."

"Don't worry. I have everything under control." Then in a lower conspiratorial voice, Tamara added, "Not sure if you do."

Piper said nothing. She didn't have control. She hadn't had it since she first looked into those dark brown eyes of the new owner of the Christensen ranch. In a short forty-eight hours, she'd become used to rushing over to Cal's in the morning and spending the day with him and his family. Now they were gone and she needed to get back to her own routine. They had a project to complete and it needed her full and undivided attention.

As if on cue, a truck turned into the driveway.

"Time for me to go," Tamara said, uncurling herself from the railing. Piper reached for the coffee cup she held.

"Tamara." Piper stopped her as she started down the steps. Tamara turned back.

"I just want to say thank you for keeping things on track."

"Courtship does require time," she said. "Especially when you're at the meet-the-family stage. And besides—" she leaned closer and lowered her voice "—I love bossing people around."

Laughing, Tamara went down the steps and headed toward the parking truck. Piper went inside, dropped the empty cup in the kitchen sink and left by the back door. Her horse Silver was waiting. Putting her foot in the stirrup, she swung her body over the horse and sat tall as she turned the animal toward Cal's ranch. It was time to face him without the buffer of his brother and sister-in-law between them.

While Tamara had teased her about courting, her weekend with Cal had changed their relationship. She needed to get it back to *work* only. Piper had loved the dancing and the good times. It was like a release for all the pent-up emotion she'd been holding. But now she had to go back to where she'd been. There was no moving forward for them. Cal had mentioned that he had good job offers he was considering. They both had important goals and ones that didn't complement each other.

Jumping down from Silver, Piper raced up the steps and into the kitchen. The mixed aromas had her stomach yearning even though she'd already eaten.

"He's in there," Naomi said, gesturing toward the office, never even looking up.

Piper guessed he was already back to business. She wondered if he'd changed after his brother's visit. Yet she didn't know what change she wanted or expected. She wished she could ask Naomi what kind of mood he was in, but that would be another line she wasn't ready to cross.

Piper knocked on the open door and went inside as Cal glanced up.

"Ready to get back to it?" he asked. Cal stood up and came around the desk.

That answered her question about his mood. She could tell by his body language that he was the before-the-weekend Cal.

She nodded, wondering if she could be the before-the-weekend Piper.

"Tamara seems to have everything under

control on the supplies and building front. I'm surprised at how much has been done since we started."

"It does seem to go fast when everything arrives on time and all the pieces fall in place."

Cal never stopped being an engineer, Piper thought. She liked that about him. He could talk about anything, but his world revolved around putting things together in the proper order. It didn't matter if it was on the computer screen, in his head or actual pieces of metal. Everything had a place, an order, a reason for being. She was glad he was on her team.

Together they had laid out every detail that needed to be checked and rechecked. Everyone had a job, and as professionals, they performed them flawlessly. Even the students from the local film schools worked alongside mentors they never expected to know.

Piper wanted everything to be the same as it had been on that day, the one that threw her future into disarray. Even the time of day and direction of the sun had to be exact. The structure, which looked like two giant metal beasts rising toward the sun, was coming together.

"Have you heard from them?" Piper asked.

Cal faced her. "They arrived in New York City late last night."

Piper hesitated a long time before saying, "I miss them."

Cal took a step toward her but stopped short of crossing into her personal space. "I miss them, too."

Piper thought her reactions to Cal would be familiar by now, but they weren't. Heat tingled across her face and body, yet there was always some new emotion, connected to him, that sprang to life without her knowing it existed. While he spoke of his brother and sister-in-law, Piper couldn't help hearing something different and personal in his voice.

Should she believe it?

Piper woke from a restless sleep. She'd been awake most of the night, reviewing what Cal had said, how he'd said it. By the time she actually fell asleep, she had no answers. Her phone rang, jarring her, and she lunged for it, wanting more to stop the noise than discover who was on the other end of the line. She pushed at the screen light, not caring if she hit accept or decline.

"Hello," she said, her voice husky as she turned over in bed. What time was it? It was still dark. The only light in the room came from the phone.

"Tell me you aren't trying to build that scaffolding."

Piper sat straight up in bed. She hadn't heard that voice in over a year, but she knew exactly who it was.

"Xavier!" She couldn't keep her surprise at bay.

"Haven't you had enough misery in your life? You want to bring this whole thing up again? Or do you have a death wish and just want to kill yourself or someone else?" Xavier was almost shouting.

Piper didn't answer. She knew when Xavier got on a roll, it was better to let him get it all out, rather than interrupting. She had plenty to say, so she'd wait. Glancing at the clock, the digital numbers read three thirty-seven. That meant it was an hour earlier on the West Coast.

"Are you finished?" she asked after a beat of silence passed.

"Piper, this is serious," he said.

"I agree. I've been over and over the video for more than a year and I don't see where I did anything wrong." She forced herself not to shout.

"Well, we both know that's not true."

Piper's teeth clinched at the pain of his words. She'd known this conversation would take place eventually, as soon as she'd agreed with Cal to go ahead with the planning. She was calmer than she thought she'd be when she and Xavier had their final confrontation. She had to be. Xavier loved to have the last word. And her revisiting the accident hit close to home for him.

"One way or the other, I'll know the truth," she told him. "I've second-guessed myself long enough. I'm going to find out what *really* happened." She emphasized the word because, despite his accusation, she didn't believe she'd done anything wrong. And because she had to know. Whether she was wrong or right, she had to know.

"You can't be sure of that," Xavier said, his voice a little stronger than before. "The court found it inconclusive. What could you hope to find?"

His comment was condescending, but Piper had hardened herself to his outbursts. It was because of him that she had doubts.

"Xavier." She used a strong voice to counter his. "This is my call. The setup was mine. The design was mine. As you so often pointed out, the entire project was mine. I no longer work for you, so you have no say in anything I do."

He started to talk again, repeating what he'd said before.

"Good night, Xavier. Or good morning. I'm hanging up now."

He was still talking when she clicked the button on the phone to end the call. Then she turned it off, so if he called back, it wouldn't disturb her. But her night had been ruined. It was doubtful that she'd get back to sleep. He probably called her in the middle of the night for just that reason.

And it worked. Her heart was beating double time. Doubt crept into her thoughts. She could be wrong. So far, she had no proof that she could find the answer she wanted. Suppose she found out that the truth was exactly what he said it was. What would she do then? Cal said he believed in her, but neither of them knew for sure.

Getting up, she pulled a wrap on over her gown and went to the kitchen. She wished Tamara was up to talk to and there was fresh coffee already made.

Popping a single-serve coffee pod in the machine, she brewed a cup of vanilla-flavored coffee. She needed the sugar, she told herself. Something to take the edge off Xavier's words.

There was a full moon and Piper went out on the porch and took a seat. As many times as she'd watched the video and seen the metal monster in her nightmares, it now sat a quarter of a mile away. It felt closer in the darkness. Moonlight bounced off the gray metal, giving it an eerie quality. It mocked her, daring her to climb it. She could almost hear it laughing through an unfinished yet gaping mouth. Its ugliness somehow projecting an unexpected beauty against the moonlit sky, hiding the fact that a devil lay in wait.

Was he right? Piper asked herself. Could Xavier know the truth? Cal had called in favors to help her. She'd gotten volunteers from the schools. The town had come to her aid. Even some of her friends in Hollywood had made the trip to Montana. Was it all for nothing?

"Having trouble sleeping?" Tamara's voice was soft and cautious.

Piper looked over her shoulder to see her friend walking forward. She was also holding a cup of coffee.

"You, too?" Piper asked.

Tamara nodded.

"I didn't really think this was going to come together when Cal first suggested it," Piper said. "Seeing it…" She glanced at the scaffolding.

"It's daunting," Tamara finished for her.

Tamara moved around, leaning against the porch railing and facing Piper.

"Have you thought this operation all the way through?" she asked.

Piper stared at her. She knew what Tamara meant.

"You could get hurt or even killed," she continued. "Austin knew that stunt backward and forward. He'd practiced it over and over, and he still fell almost to his death. Are you sure you want to do it?"

Piper could see the concern on Tamara's face even in the half light of the morning. She leaned forward, setting her cup down on the small table next to her chair.

"I won't lie to you. I have concerns. There's no definitive information to show what happened to Austin. Even he doesn't remember anything going wrong."

After Austin was finally able to talk, he couldn't remember the accident. While the doctors said that was normal and would pass, to this day, he still had no memory of the details of his fall.

"Even today, Austin can't remember anything about the accident." Tamara echoed Piper's thoughts. "He may never remember. But we don't want to repeat that with you."

Piper stood up, taking several steps away from Tamara. She turned and faced her. "Xavier called tonight."

"What?" Tamara came away from the railing. Her cup teetered, but she caught it before it fell. Coffee spilled onto her hand. She wiped it on her nightgown, saying nothing about it being hot.

"He gave me all the rhetoric about killing myself, being a fool, bringing up old wounds that are better left in the past, everything I've already told myself." She waved her arm as if encompassing Xavier's entire litany of warnings.

"That's why you're out here?"

"He still gets to me. I knew I wasn't going to get back to sleep after the call. I finally just hung up and turned the phone off. I knew he was bound to hear about this. With so many of the crew members who have worked with him before and are here volunteering, it was inevitable."

"He probably feels like you're taking control and you know how he hates that," Tamara said, her voice showing a little humor. "You're bringing back memories he'd rather forget. That accident is a blemish on his record, his company, and caused him a huge financial hit. It's still teetering."

"His blemish is nowhere near the size of mine," Piper defended. "Still, I took some of what he said and what you've said about the danger as things I should be concerned about."

"You know there are plenty of stunt workers willing to do this."

"It's hard to face, but if I'm ever going to get past this stigma, I have to know the truth. I can't allow anyone else to do the stunt. I so appreciate the volunteers who said they would do it, but if I truly want to realize what occurred, I'm the only one who can do that. And I can't put someone else's life in danger. My experience level is the closest to that of Austin's. If I don't do it, I'll never have an answer."

"And you're willing to risk your life on that?"

Piper smiled quickly. "We risk our lives every day to do what we do. We know we have to be extra cautious to make sure the outcome is positive."

"And we know that about this one, too," Tamara reminded her.

Piper walked to the banister. Planting her hands on the cold wood and staring at the scaffolding, she mentally challenged it to give her the answer. "We've done the work. We have the specs." She looked at Tamara. "With the help of all the schools and one of the studios in Hollywood where I still have some clout, we have more cameras than we did on the original job. If anything goes wrong, we'll know. But…" She stood up straight, putting her hand up, palm out, stopping Tamara from saying anything. "Nothing is going to go wrong."

"Well, just remember, none of us really has nine lives," Tamara cautioned. "We get one and only one. Let's make sure it lasts."

AIMLESSNESS WAS SOMETHING Cal rarely experienced. Since his weekend with his brother, sister-in-law and Piper, however, he spent long periods of time doing nothing but staring at the distant rise near her house. Meanwhile, the work progressed to set up the stunt. Piper had pointed out that they were further along than either of them expected. With each new section completed, Cal became more and more nervous of the outcome. While he'd worked the engineering mathematics and knew everything should perform without a hitch, there was still both the unknown element and the human factor that could not be predicted.

Piper was that factor.

Cal was afraid for her. It wasn't a lack

of confidence. She was the most competent person he'd met in a long time. She knew her job. She was fit and strong. And he had no doubt that she could perform the stunt, but Austin had been hurt. He could have been killed. Closing his eyes at the thought, he quickly opened them, chasing away the image of her tumbling to the ground. Something unforeseen had gone wrong in Austin's stunt and that was a factor that could cause her to be hurt. Cal couldn't stomach that. Suppose something happened. Suppose he missed a calculation or made a wrong assumption.

He knew there was no talking her out of it, even if he was inclined to try, which he wasn't. She'd been dragging this angst around for almost two years. Instead of it getting lighter, it was weighing her down. He didn't want to add any more doubts to the ones she must have. From his own experiences, he knew a positive attitude could be the difference between success and failure.

"You've been wearing the floor out for a couple days now. What are you thinking?" Naomi asked as she packed supplies for the crew's morning meal. "That wrinkled brow is a dead giveaway."

Cal looked away from the windows, unaware that he had an expression on his face.

"Don't try to hide it. I know you're worried about her."

"You know, Naomi, I wonder if my mother would mind that you are usurping her role."

"She's not here and I am," Naomi said. "But I know she'd agree with me."

Cal grunted rather than laughed. His mother wouldn't exactly approve, but she would approve Naomi's intentions.

"Seriously," Naomi said, concern in her voice. "I know you think something can go wrong and Piper will be hurt. You've worked every angle and that woman Tamara isn't letting anything get past her."

Cal nodded. Even though Naomi referred to Tamara as *that woman*, she really admired Tamara. "There's still that human factor, right? It's the one percent we can't control."

"Piper can." Naomi was positive in her statement. "Now, let's get this over to the site."

They packed his truck and rode over together. Piper and Tamara were hard at it when they arrived. Cal dropped Naomi in the eating area and continued to the small trailer they used as a command center.

"It looks like more progress has been made since yesterday," he said, coming up behind Piper.

"I think they'll be finished tonight. Practically everything is ready. Even the weather forecast is on our side."

The expected response should be *great*, but Cal refused to say it. "Have you tested your equipment?" he asked instead, even though he knew the answer.

She nodded. "Tamara insisted that I go through every buckle so she could see that nothing was out of place."

"She's going to be fine when she opens her own business," Cal said with admiration.

"I agree. If this test goes well, my reputation in this world will be restored."

"Really? Are you sure?" Cal remembered how harshly she'd spoken of her time after the accident.

"With all these people here, word was bound to get back to the studios that I'm re-creating this stunt. I've had several phone calls. A week from Friday, I expect a few stunt company executives will be here."

"Does this mean you'll be moving back to California?"

Piper looked over the site. She turned slowly, completing a full circle before her gaze settled on him. "I suppose it will. My work is there. And I told you Tamara asked me to go in with her on a new venture."

"I thought you'd decided against that."

"I had. But if things change, I adapt. I'm hoping for the best. If it goes awry, I'll still have to adapt to something."

For some reason, Cal didn't like that answer. They'd worked together for several weeks on her project. He'd become used to her company. She complemented him with her knowledge and strength. He enjoyed talking to her without having to explain everything. Cal knew her goal was to get back to the life she loved, the one she'd left behind, but he wasn't ready for it to come so abruptly.

He'd said he wanted to go back to his life, too, but... He couldn't finish that sentence. Things had changed for him. *She* had caused that change. He didn't have that longing to get on a plane and fly off to some remote area and build a bridge or oversee a tunnel. He liked horseback riding with her. He liked waking up each day knowing he'd see her and the two of them would spend time together.

He had feelings for Piper like he'd never had for anyone else.

And while they scared him, he didn't want them to go away.

Not just yet—or ever.

CAL HADN'T BEEN able to sleep. That the human factor was something he couldn't control and could get Piper hurt, plagued his nights. Finally getting up, he paced the floor, walking in aimless circles. Stopping, he looked at his hands as if there was something that should be in them but wasn't. Phone, he thought.

Grabbing his cell, he quickly checked the time and hit one of the quick dial codes. Jake answered on the first ring.

"Hi," Jake said, a smile in his voice. "I've been expecting your call."

"I'm not catching you on your way to surgery, am I?"

"Not today," Jake said.

Then what his brother said registered. "What do you mean, you've been expecting my call?"

"It must be close to *go time* by now," Jake said. "When does she perform the stunt?"

Cal's mouth twisted, but he couldn't call it a smile. "This weekend. How did you know?"

"You're worried about her," Jake stated. "I could see it the moment she rode up to us on that ridge. And I'm sure she's concerned about you, too."

Cal blinked and sat down. He didn't know what to say. He hadn't seen any sign recently that Piper wanted anything more from him than friendship. There had been their kiss, but they'd reverted to just friends after that. Maybe his definition of friendship was different from Jake's.

"I'm afraid, Jake," Cal admitted. "Suppose something goes wrong."

"It's not going to. You've done the calculations, right?"

"Six ways from Sunday," Cal replied.

"And you're confident that they are right?"

"Without a doubt."

"Then you have nothing to worry about," Jake comforted him.

"There's the unknown factor," Cal repeated. "Numbers don't tell you everything."

He knew Jake was aware of what he meant. No matter how many numbers he crunched or how aware he was that everything was correct according to the math and physics, there was the unknown. It was what Piper would do when she started the run. Would she connect with the pipes at the right time? Would the pounding on the structure perform the same as it had the day before? Would her tie-rope get caught on something? The humidity, the wind, the sunlight were all variables he'd calculated, but he couldn't tell how she would see the area in front of her, how she would react to any obstacle, real or imagined, as she rushed through the framework.

"Cal, are you still there?"

Jake's voice pulled his attention back to the call. "I'm here."

"I understand what you're thinking. Surgery is the same. No matter how many times I've done the same procedure, something can always go wrong."

"The difference is you're there with a team

of specialists to make corrections. Piper is going to be up there all alone. No matter how many technicians are on the ground, she'll be on her own."

"No, she won't," Jake contradicted. "She'll have years of experience behind her. She'll have a body that is strong and capable. She'll have the previous practices behind her. And she'll have the support of all her friends, including you. Especially you."

Cal thought about that. While his brother's words were true, they only reduced Cal's anxiety by a fraction.

"You have to let her go," Jake said, his voice almost a whisper. "She is who she is. That's why you fell in love with her, isn't it?"

Cal had never said he was in love with Piper. Not to her and not to his brother. But he and Jake were on the same page these days. Just as Cal had read Jake's love for Lauren, he was sure his brother understood his feelings for Piper.

"You *are* in love with her." Jake didn't ask. He stated it as fact.

"Fully and completely," Cal answered.

"WHAT'S THIS?" Piper asked, coming into the dining room at Cal's place the following evening. She expected another working evening like all the others they'd had. Tonight was obviously different.

She surveyed the room and looked questioningly at Cal. There were flowers and lit candles on the table, which was laid with only two place settings. And whatever she was smelling focused her attention on how little she had eaten in the last twenty-four hours.

"You did this for me?"

"I told you I often have to fend for myself," Cal replied.

Piper looked toward the kitchen. "Where's Naomi?"

"She's not here tonight."

"You did this?" she said again. "This is a little more than fending. I feel like I should be dressed in a gown with my hair in curls." Her hand went to her head and she brushed her untoward hair away from her face.

Cal's gaze followed the movement of her hands.

"Your hair looks fine," he said. She was lost in the tone of his voice. The moment was mesmerizing. She felt stuck, transfixed in one spot. She couldn't move but knew she had to.

"What are we eating?" she was finally able to ask.

"Sit down. It's my specialty," Cal told her.

"You have a specialty?" She took a seat, happy to be able to take her weight off knees she was unsure would continue to support her.

"Doesn't everyone?"

Cal went to the kitchen. Piper looked over the dining room again. The space was romantically appointed, perfect lighting designed to convey a mood. It was a set, she told herself, put together by an experienced decorator. And it was serving its purpose. Piper felt relaxed and appreciated that someone was doing something for her without being asked or expecting anything in return.

Sitting back, she watched as Cal put a plate in front of her.

"It smells delicious," she said, taking in the aroma of slow-cooked barbecue. "Is that homemade bread?"

Cal handed her the basket of warm rolls.

Piper inhaled, her eyes closing as if she'd never smelled anything as delicious as this. When Cal took a seat across from her, she took a bite of the falling-off-the-bone meat.

"These are the best ribs I've ever tasted."

"Well, you are in Montana," he said.

THEY WERE BACK to their old routine of working day and night. Cal had enjoyed being with Piper. Afterward, the two always seemed to exchange a look that said they had a secret. He knew it was friendship.

The work never seemed to stop. They had a deadline and Cal tried to concentrate, but he was more and more distracted by Piper. He had to check his feelings, keep them inside, when he wanted to let her know that he was attracted to her.

At the end of the week, Piper met him for breakfast at the diner.

"Why don't we take the day off tomorrow?" Cal said.

"What?" Piper stared at him.

Her eyes were tired, along with her posture. She could hardly keep her eyes open.

"We've been hard at this for weeks. You're tired. Our brains need a rest. We'll get a good night's sleep and spend the day doing something that has nothing to do with recreating the stunt. Deal?"

She hesitated a moment. Cal knew she

was weighing their options. They had a finite deadline. A day and time when all the puzzle pieces would fit in place. At least, Piper hoped they would. She just had to be patient. And they *were* tired.

"Being tired leads to mistakes and oversights. We can come back the day after with fresh minds."

"Do you think we can afford a day off?" she asked.

"I don't think we can continue without it."

She thought for a long moment.

"Piper," Cal prompted.

"Agreed," she said.

Cal was relived. "What would you like to do?"

"I have one lesson in the morning. My second student canceled. After that, I'm free."

"How about we explore the area?"

"On horseback?" she asked.

"Not on horseback," Cal countered. He was thinking of driving someplace very different and spending the day. "Your go-to method is to stay away from people. I vote we do the opposite this time. And if we go into town, people will see us and we'll be talking and not spending as much time together. Right? You've made a lot of friends since Meghan's party and the project got underway."

"I have made quite a few friends."

"You have," he said quietly. "Friends and family are the most important things you have in life. You should never push them away."

Piper's chin came up as she stared directly at him.

"I believe in being straightforward," she said.

"I hadn't noticed," he teased. Cal had learned that about her. "I'll forgo my lesson tomorrow and we can leave right after your first student is done."

"All right," she said. "Now, what do you recommend for breakfast here?"

Piper was facing Cal in the booth and his hand naturally fell to the table beside hers. He slipped his hand in hers. It was for support, he told himself. They were both exhausted and it felt right that they should start the day this way. Piper didn't shrug him off or move to avoid his touch.

And he liked that.

SHE SHOULD HAVE asked what Cal had in mind, Piper thought the next morning as she tried to find something to wear. So often she was in riding clothes that she didn't think much about regular day-to-day dressing. Her lesson had gone well and had finished a little early, since the rider was with one of her best students. She knew what to do and had practiced perfecting her technique.

Now Piper's bedroom looked like an explosion in a clothing factory. She'd changed outfits four times, not to mention the jeans, dresses and blouses she'd pulled out and discarded. This would take hours to tidy up. She didn't even know why she was making such an issue of what to wear. This wasn't a date. It was two people taking a breather after weeks of work.

Lifting a hanger with a red sweater that matched white pants, she held it up to herself and looked in the full-length mirror. Shaking her head, she threw it on top of the collection of rejects on the bed.

She didn't want to wear pants. Cal always saw her in pants. Picking several dresses, she finally decided on a pink-and-white sundress. It floated over her head and fit snugly to her waist. Then it flared out slightly about her legs. Surveying herself in the mirror, she thought if she was going to try to look extra pretty, she may as well dress the part. Leaving her hair free, she heard Cal's truck. Too late to change anything, she applied a little lipstick and slipped her feet into flat sandals. Taking a last check of her hair and grabbing a sweater, she skipped down the stairs, her heart racing at knowing he was here.

At the bottom of the staircase, she stopped, taking a breath and reminding herself that she was acting like a sixteen-year-old going on her first date. Slowly, she walked to the door as the bell began its eight-note chime. Cal had his back to her when she pulled the door inward. He turned.

"Wow," he said.

Piper blushed. She felt a secret thrill run through her that he liked the way she looked. Pushing down the thought that this wasn't a date, she glanced down at herself, then back at him. Cal wore a button-down white shirt with an open collar and khaki pants.

"I didn't know where we were going," she

explained, indicating her clothing. "I hope this is all right."

"It's good for anything except horseback riding."

They both laughed. It seemed to break the tension that had built within her. She let out a breath. "I'll get my purse," she said.

Moments later they were in his truck. She noticed it had been cleaned inside and out and had a fresh smell. Smiling, she allowed herself to think he'd done it for her, although she couldn't imagine when he'd had the time.

"Where are we going?" she asked when he turned onto the road leading into Waymon Valley.

"I thought we'd have lunch at Taurus. I've never been there before, but Naomi recommends it. Have you ever been there?"

Piper shook her head.

The restaurant wasn't so much on her mind as the feeling that passed along her skin from his touch. Yesterday he'd slipped his arm around her as they walked. She liked the feel of it. The gesture was comforting, but more than that, she wanted to nestle into him. Wanted to move closer to Cal.

They passed the rest of the drive in companionable silence. Entering the town limits of Waymon Valley was like seeing the black-and-white world in *The Wizard of Oz* change to color.

Buildings sprang up of various heights and facades.

Cal pulled into the last empty parking space beside the restaurant. Since the lot was full, she assumed that the dining room would be completely occupied.

It was.

But Cal had a reservation and they were shown directly to a table near the massive windows that looked out on a picturesque view.

"Greetings, folks. You've got here just in time. About to run out of our specialty—prime rib and home-baked corn bread." The waiter handed them menus. "Now, if you'd like something special, not on our menu, Ms. Logan, you just let me know."

"Do I know you?" she asked.

"News travels fast in these parts. I'm Manuel." His head bowed slightly. "As far as you're concerned, your celebrity precedes you."

Both she and Cal glanced at the gold plate on his maroon jacket. When their drink order was taken and he retreated, they both let out a loud laugh. Cal said, "Gee, I'm with a big star. If I'd known, I'd have put on my better boots."

She laughed at his joke, loving how easily he could read her and what she needed. Thinking of reading, Piper wondered if she was reading more into this than what was there. She reminded herself this was not a date, despite her many changes of clothes and the way she felt when he greeted her with the one word that every woman wants to hear—*Wow!*

Piper tried to calm the butterflies, but she couldn't. People were whispering to each other and she didn't miss the surreptitious looks sent in her direction. She was sure the story of her time in Hollywood was known by everyone there.

"They're not staring at you." Cal spoke lowly as if he could read her thoughts. "They're admiring you."

She glanced at him.

"You're the most incredible woman. You should expect stares."

Piper smiled, embracing the moment. Did he really think she was incredible? She looked at the menu to hide the smile on her face. Cal pulled it down.

"Don't hide," he said. "You should be seen."

She started to smile, but just then out of the corner of her eye, she saw two women get up and start for their table. Piper gripped the menu a little harder, willing them to pass by and go toward the exit.

No luck.

They stopped right at her table. She looked up. One had salt-and-pepper hair and wore a pretty green suit. She looked a little embarrassed. Probably not as embarrassed as Piper would look when they asked about her plight on the set of a Hollywood movie.

The other younger woman must be her daughter. The two looked enough alike to be related.

"Pardon me, but aren't you Piper Logan?"

Caught, Piper thought. "I am."

"We hate to bother you," the older one said. "But would you mind autographing this? We love seeing you as Elisabeth Grey, especially knowing you're from Waymon Valley."

She gestured toward the paper and pen she held in hand.

"I'd be happy to," Piper said.

Both women smiled and handed her the paper.

"What are your names?"

Piper made out the autographs to them and watched as they returned to their table all smiles.

She looked at Cal, who was smirking.

"What?" she asked.

"Baby steps," he replied.

THE FOOD COULDN'T have been better, Cal thought as they finished the meal and headed out. He pulled the door of the truck open. Piper slid inside.

"Now, that wasn't so bad, was it?" Cal asked, shifting gears and pulling onto the county road. Instead of heading back toward town, Cal turned the truck in the opposite direction and went farther down the county road.

"I agree, it wasn't bad."

The two women had set the mood and Piper had seemed to finally relax enough to enjoy the meal. Cal was happy about that and was ready for the next part of his plan, hoping Piper was up for it, too.

"Where are we going?" Piper asked when they crossed the city limits but didn't turn back toward either his ranch or hers.

"It's a surprise," Cal said.

"I'm not—"

"I know you're not used to that," Cal interrupted. "But for a few minutes, let someone else have control."

"You think I'm a control freak?"

"In a good way," he answered. "You pay close attention to detail and organize every aspect of, well, everything. It's an admirable attribute."

"Thank you. I've never been described in such a positive way and negative way at the same time," Piper said.

"It's not negative."

She put her hand up to stop him. "I appreciate it. I even agree with it."

Cal drove on. The wide-open space and the rise and fall of the land allowed them to see for miles. In the distance, there was one place that rose like a mirage.

"An amusement park!" Piper exclaimed.

Cal smiled but didn't say anything. He

continued to negotiate the twists and turns until they reached the entry gate.

"I haven't been to an amusement park in…" She stopped. "I can't remember the last time I was at one."

"It's been years for me, too," he said.

"I wonder if they still have funnel cake."

"Cake? You just finished eating."

"You don't have cake because you're hungry. It's pure delight and I didn't have dessert."

"I thought you were too full."

"No one is ever too full for funnel cake," she said.

He parked and she practically pulled him along, she walked so fast.

"Have you ever had funnel cake?" Piper asked.

"Once or twice."

Cal was enjoying this new Piper Logan. He'd seen the efficient woman, the expert horsewoman, even the sad troubled woman, but this playful, wide-eyed, young woman was richly different and as multidimensional as all the others. He'd like to get to know this one, too.

"What would you like to do first?" Cal asked.

"Everything," she shouted, spreading her arms and spinning around in a full circle, her dress flaring out.

They couldn't do everything at once. Cal decided to start slow. He headed toward the merry-go-round. Piper's fingers curled around his upper arm and rushed him to the roller coaster instead.

"You're not afraid of falling, are you?" she asked.

"From that?" He indicated the giant orange complex of metal and lights. "With its sharp drop, dips and loops, countered by squeals of laughter and fright. Am I afraid of that? You bet your life."

"Good, let's go. We can start with the small one," Piper suggested.

The small one had a ninety-degree drop, three full 360-degree loops and multiple tilt-angle turns. The line was short for such a beautiful summer afternoon. It was Wednesday and should be more crowded, since schoolkids were out for vacation.

The roller coaster climbed slowly. Cal could count the gears as they locked into and out of each one. The car crawled upward like a tortoise until it reached the zenith. For the space of five seconds, it tethered on the crest. Heightening both anticipation and fear, the car moved inch by inch until it completed the summit, then plunged headlong down the tracks.

Screams went up, Piper's along with everyone else's. She grabbed Cal and held on. Her hair obscured his vision. Slipping his arm around her shoulders, he pulled her as close as the safety rail allowed. The jerking car pushed and pulled them, but he held her as tight as he could. He didn't want to let her go. Finally, the car arrived back at the beginning, slowing on a cushion of air. Reluctantly, Cal eased his arms and pushed back.

"Wasn't that amazing?" Piper said. "I haven't done that in a long time."

"The last time I was at an amusement park, I was in college. Right after graduation, I got my first job and there was no time for anything else," Cal said as they left the ride.

They walked along the main strip leading to another ride.

"Where was that?" Piper asked.

"My first job?"

She nodded.

"An offshore oil rig. I was one of the junior engineers. We lived on it once it was floated."

"Wow!"

Cal thought she was impressed with his job, but as she rushed away, he saw she was interested in one of the food stations.

"French fried apples. Have you ever had them?"

"Not that I can remember."

For the next several hours, they rushed from one ride to another, eating in between, everything from cotton candy to cheese on a stick and, of course, funnel cake. Hours rushed by without them even thinking about time. Finally, they sat in the food tent eating their cake.

"One more ride before we need to head back," Cal said, watching Piper drop a torn-off piece of cake into her mouth.

"Why? I'm not tired," Piper said.

"This was supposed to be a relaxing day. We don't want to be wiped out tomorrow," he said.

"It's been so much fun." She grinned. "I'm glad you thought of it."

"We can always come back again," he told her. In fact, he'd like to come back with her. But he knew they were working together toward a goal, and once that was complete, they would go their separate ways. He'd probably choose another job that took him out of the country. And depending on the success or failure of her project, she would return to her world or embark on another career.

If her project failed, she'd need time to come to terms with what to do with the rest of her life. They both had decisions to make. But not now. Now, they needed to go on their last amusement ride.

"What one do you want to go on?" Piper asked.

"We've been on practically all of them. Since we started with a bang, why don't we end with something less frightening—the Ferris wheel?"

"Some people are terribly frightened of being that high off the ground. Especially with nothing around them, like an airplane," Piper said.

"But you're not one of them," Cal stated.

"Nope." She stood up and the two of them hurried like kids to the big wheel.

LOCKED IN, the Ferris wheel seat began to swing. The sun was long from setting, but it had moved across the sky. As they reached the top, Piper looked around at the vast area they could see. The mountains were the best feature, she thought.

"I love those mountains. In Los Angeles, you never see the mountains, only hills and they are filled with houses. Here, the place is so open. Inviting."

"That was one of the selling points for me to buy the Christensen ranch. I loved it that the sky was so close and full of stars at night." He looked up to emphasize the point. There would be stars later. Now the setting sun was painting the sky dark blues and reds.

The seat swung faster, and Piper jumped slightly. She wasn't afraid of heights, but the movement was a little unsettling, especially after all the food she'd consumed.

"I once saw a movie, an old one." Cal smiled. "About two kids on a Ferris wheel."

"Remembering a scene like this one?" she asked.

"Sort of." He tightened his arm around her shoulders. She leaned into it.

"So what happened in the movie?" she asked.

"I don't remember the name of it, but there were two awkward kids—about ten or eleven years old."

"Boy meets girl?" She smiled.

"You guessed it." He shifted in the swinging seat.

"So what did this awkward eleven-year-old do on the Ferris wheel?" Piper prompted.

"He kissed the girl."

Piper was speechless. She had nothing to say. The instance took her back to Meghan asking if Cal had kissed her good-night. Emotions overtook her, holding her still.

"It was the first kiss, for each of them," he continued, unaware of the corkscrew of awareness that spiraled through her.

"I see," she whispered, still looking at him. Piper wanted to pull her gaze away, but she couldn't. For long moments neither of them moved or spoke. Not even when his face began to move closer to hers did she retreat. He was going to kiss her. She wanted it. She'd known that she had wanted him to kiss her good-night after their dinner. And she knew that she wanted it now.

Suddenly the seat jerked, and instead of a kiss, they bumped heads. "Ouch," Piper said, her hand going to the point of impact. The car stopped. They were back at the beginning of the ride. The wheel attendant unclasped the locked bar to let them out.

"Are you all right?" Cal asked.

Piper smiled. "More embarrassed than hurt."

"Let me see."

He didn't wait for her to approve. Pushing her hair aside, he checked her forehead.

"No bruises," he announced.

She felt Cal's hand on her brow. It slid down her cheek. A sound behind them had Cal standing and guiding her toward the exit.

"The timing wasn't right anyway," he said.

When Piper smiled, Cal did, too.

Following their fellow riders, they walked down the ramp and exited the area.

"With that, I guess it is time we returned to the ranches," Piper said.

Cal reached for her hand. Piper put hers in his before she even thought about it. They started walking. The crowd had increased since they arrived. Piper understood it was a good idea with such a large group of people around them—holding hands was the best way to keep from losing each other. And she thought Cal was making sure her head injury wasn't serious. That was the logical reason for him to keep her near. Piper preferred the nonlogical one—that he just wanted to hold her hand.

CAL COULDN'T HELP smiling as he glanced at Piper. She insisted she wasn't tired, yet ten minutes into the drive back to the ranch, she'd fallen asleep. Her head bobbed until he reached across and settled her against his shoulder. He liked the way she felt. He liked that she felt comfortable enough with him to let go of her need to control everything. She'd been working hard, and even though the day was fun, it was tiring, too. But it was the good kind of tired.

It wasn't long before Cal turned into the driveway leading to Piper's ranch. She didn't open her eyes when he stopped the truck.

For a long moment, Cal let her lie against him. Releasing both their seat belts, she slumped farther, this time moving her arm across his waist. Cal took in a long breath and held it. His eyes closed and he rested his head against hers. He would only do it for a moment or two.

Almost a half hour later, he was still holding her and on his own way to falling asleep. Piper moved and jolted him awake. She opened her eyes and they sat up together, pulling back as if they were surprised to find themselves in each other's arms.

"We're here," she said groggily. Her voice reminded him of morning. "Sorry, I didn't mean to fall asleep." She yawned and, using her fingertips, wiped the sleep from the corners of her eyes. It was a simple gesture, but Cal wanted to take her hands away and use his own to banish the sleep from her eyes.

Instead, he opened the door. The temperature had dropped and it was much cooler than it had been during the day. He welcomed the fresh air. Getting out, he walked around to where Piper had already opened her door. He reached up and helped her down. While they'd held hands for most of the day, they didn't touch each other as they mounted the steps to her front door.

Piper turned to him. "I know this is a line that someone is supposed to say after a day like today, but I had a *really* nice time."

"We'll have to do it again," Cal suggested.

"I'd like that."

Cal leaned forward and kissed her on the cheek. He wanted to go further, but didn't. Piper had returned to Montana after a bad relationship and Cal assumed she wasn't ready for another one just yet.

"See you tomorrow," he said.

"Not too early. I might sleep in."

"Me, too."

With a short wave, he returned to the truck. She watched him from the porch until he turned around the circular driveway and headed back to the road.

It had been a good day. Cal couldn't remember when he'd enjoyed himself more. He felt like a kid again, learning all about a woman he was attracted to. But one with whom his time was running short.

His house was quiet when he entered it. It wasn't very late, but he'd had a long day— one where he'd held hands with Piper and almost kissed her. Mounting the stairs one slow foot at a time, Cal got to his room and fell asleep the moment he got into bed. He woke with the sounds of Naomi bustling in the kitchen and the smell of the best coffee on the planet. Despite yesterday's fun, he was wide awake and ready to get back to work. He wondered if Piper was awake yet and if she felt like he did.

It struck him then that she was his first thought out of bed. And she'd been his last thought before he went to sleep. Cal couldn't deny his feelings were changing toward Piper. He couldn't wait to see her each day. He and Piper usually began with his riding lesson and then breakfast, but the aroma coming from the kitchen and the sunlight coming in his windows told him it was well past breakfast.

BY NOON ON MONDAY, the framework for the re-creation was finished and everything was in place. The crew started the cleanup, moving debris and unused supplies to a safe location out of the way. The cleanup would take the rest of the day. From her perch high above the ground, Piper checked several connections, giving the crew a thumbs-up signal each time. Spying Cal on the ground, she stopped. He was hunched over his laptop, probably going over measurements and calculations, running scenarios. She smiled. He worked all the time, making sure there was no contingency that he'd overlooked.

She liked that about him, that he was always thinking of her safety. She even liked that he could read her moods, understand when she needed a break and stand by her, giving her his strength but never trying to make her decisions for her.

Tamara was in the air, too. She and a pair of crew members, experienced in construction testing, looked over the equipment, inspecting it section by section for weight, balance, wind adjustment, loose connections, temperature increases and decreases, and any other factors that could affect a positive outcome.

Looking for Cal again, Piper waved to him as he shaded his eyes and waved back at her. Grabbing one of the aerial hoops, she gently lowered herself to the ground.

"How's it feel?" he asked when she released the huge circle and stepped onto solid ground.

"Perfect," she said. "I didn't find a single thing that was out of place and nothing unexpected." She glanced up. Tamara and the two crew were still up there.

"You looked comfortable on that ring." He indicated the aerial circus ring she'd used to get to the ground.

"I worked on circus pictures a few times. We went up and down it in practice so often, it became second nature." He started to speak, but she stopped him. "Don't worry. I won't be thinking that anything is second nature during the stunt. There are precise movements that need to be done, marks that have to be hit, and I'm going to do them with nothing else on my mind."

Piper waited. She could see the concern on Cal's face. Since the trucks began arriving with supplies and equipment, she'd noticed the lines between his eyebrows grow deeper.

"Cal," she said and hesitated. "I know you're concerned. You haven't said it." She reached up and smoothed the skin between his eyes. "It's written on your face, though."

She drew her hand back, but he caught it and held it.

"I've never seen this before," he said. "Usually, if there's something that needs fixing or checking, I'm the one on the rig."

"I get it," she told him.

He pulled her closer, resting his forehead on hers. "You can't always control everything, either. So be careful. Please."

"I will."

Piper didn't move. She was surprised she could speak. She wanted to stay where she was. She wanted all the people on the site to disappear and leave them alone. Over the previous weeks, they'd been together constantly, either on a horse or hunched over a computer working out details. She liked working with him. That was the least of it. She liked everything about him. He was easy to talk to. He listened to her when she made suggestions. Often he made her laugh and he was persistent when she tried to push him away.

Neither of them was pushing today. Piper took a step forward and hugged Cal. His arms went around her easily and stayed that way. She didn't know how long Cal hugged her, but she knew keeping her mind on the stunt and nothing else was going to be harder now that she couldn't let go of what it felt like to be his.

CAL NEEDED A few minutes alone after he left Piper. He could still feel her close to him and he wanted to hold on to that feeling, not have it taken away by conversations with the crew. Opting for the shortest distance around Piper's gym, Cal went to his house. In the kitchen, he pulled the refrigerator door open.

Surprised by what he saw, he forgot that Naomi was using the refrigerator for storing the crew's food. The shelves were stuffed from the back to the front. Cal opted for a glass of orange juice. He'd just poured it from the carton when the doorbell rang. The sound was unfamiliar. He'd become used to people calling his name and coming straight in.

Setting the glass on the counter, he went along the hallway and stopped short. He couldn't believe his eyes when he saw who stood on the other side of the screen door.

Cal's boots hit the floor hard as his stride covered the distance in three steps.

"What are you doing here?" He embraced his brother in a hug, then pulled Lauren into his arms and hugged her, too. "You two only left a few weeks ago."

"We couldn't miss the big day," Jake said as Cal ushered them into the living room. "When we left, we didn't know the exact date. We wanted to support you. And Piper."

"We'll have to impose, though," Lauren added, biting her lower lip.

"Impose?"

"Unfortunately, the hotel is full and—"

"No problem. You always have a room here," Cal interrupted. He felt as if it had been years since he saw them and their presence filled him with delight.

"How'd you get here?"

"Meghan picked us up and dropped us off," Lauren said.

Cal looked out the door.

"She had to leave but said she'd see you soon," Jake told him.

"I could have come for you."

"We wanted it to be a surprise," Jake said.

Minutes later, after Jake and Lauren had settled in and they were all in the kitchen with plates of Naomi's steaks and baked potatoes, Jake looked out toward the ridge. "It is daunting," he said.

Lauren nodded. "I didn't expect it to be so high up. Before we left, we couldn't see any of it from here. And now..."

"And now it looks like a giant metal monster," Cal tried to joke, but failed. "That's what Piper calls it."

"She must be very brave." Lauren's expression was serious.

Cal nodded. A huge lump lodged in his throat and he found it impossible to speak.

"How's she doing?" Jake asked.

"She's nervous, but determined."

Jake looked at his wife and Cal wondered if that look meant he was hoping to see Lauren offer something reassuring, too. Cal was worried. While he had suggested they recreate the circumstances of the tragic mishap, he didn't know how he'd feel when he saw that Piper would be putting her life in possible danger.

The back door opened and shut. The three

of them turned. Piper stood in the doorway for only a second before she rushed across the floor. Lauren stood and the two women hugged each other as if they hadn't just seen each other a few weeks ago.

"What are you two doing here?" She hugged Jake.

"We came to see you perform tomorrow," Lauren said.

"And I wanted the chance to see Cal again, as well," Jake said. "This time without his horse."

They all laughed. The story had been told and retold until it would follow Cal for a long time.

"Sit down and finish your meal," Piper said. "Naomi sent me in to get more drinks."

She went to the pantry and picked up a case of water.

"Whoa," Cal said. "I'll take that."

Taking the case from her, he noticed Jake had joined him, Lauren following. "How many cases does she need?" Cal asked.

"Three. I brought the truck."

"We'll get them," Cal offered, hefting the first one onto his shoulder. He headed for the door.

"I'd like to go over to the site," Lauren said.

Both Cal and Jake looked at Piper. She nodded. They all climbed into the truck and quickly covered the distance back to her ranch.

"Wow!" Jake said, once they arrived. "You did all this since we were here?" He got out of the truck, looking a little awestruck. Same for Lauren.

"It's ready," Cal confirmed, nodding.

ANY EARLY MORNING call was no surprise to Piper. She was used to it. Meghan's number appeared on her cell. Piper smiled as she answered.

"Do you know what's going on in town?" Meghan asked.

"What?"

Piper's stomach dropped as she prepared for bad news. But Meghan's voice had sounded excited.

"Everyone's talking about you and Cal."

"Me and Cal?"

The old feelings rushed back. Were they condemning her? Were they gossiping about them being a couple? She wouldn't ask. Meghan would tell her if she waited.

"Even the kids are buzzing with excitement over seeing a real Hollywood stunt."

Piper felt such relief. Her imagination had made leaps, yet it was the stunt the town was interested in. To Waymon Valley, what she was doing was real news.

"Oops," Meghan said. "Gotta go. A minor emergency in the kitchen. See you tomorrow."

She was gone before Piper could say goodbye. The town was talking, Piper thought, and they were saying good things. She sat down. Suddenly feeling as if a great weight had evaporated from her shoulders.

Putting her thoughts aside, Piper went into her final prep mode. The stunt was scheduled for the next day and there were a million details she needed to check and recheck.

The day didn't speed by as she thought it would with the constant tasks she performed. But night finally came and Cal suggested that she go to bed early. Feeling that she couldn't possibly sleep with details running through her brain like wild horses racing, she was surprised when she opened her eyes and the sun was shining.

But more surprises awaited her.

It seemed like the entire town turned out

to support Piper and watch her perform. Piper, Cal, Lauren and Jake sat at the kitchen table. Naomi was already at the site. Cal had taken to eating there recently, relieving Naomi of caring for him and the crew separately. Lauren and Jake filled in and made breakfast. They moved around his kitchen like a couple who'd worked together for years.

Piper could see people arriving in groups of threes and fours. The stream had begun a couple of hours ago. She expected some of the people from her former Hollywood community to attend. Many had called to let her know they would. But from what she could see, the entire state looked like it had emptied out. SUVs, vans and luxury cars made a parking lot of one of her fields.

There were many more people she recognized who she never thought would leave their comfortable offices in the Hollywood Hills to travel to rural Montana. Yet here they were. She wasn't sure if they'd come to see her succeed or fail.

Cal stood up and got a second cup of coffee. Walking to the huge windows, he faced

Piper's ranch. "Where did all these people come from?" he asked.

"The great state of California," Tamara answered, coming through the back door. "Good morning, everybody." She smiled at the small gathering. Going straight to the coffeepot, she poured herself a cup. "You must be Cal's brother. We didn't get to meet the last time you were here."

"You were very busy," Jake said.

"The resemblance is striking." Tamara looked from one brother to the other.

"Jake Masters," he confirmed. She shook hands with him.

"Then you must be the other Dr. Masters," Tamara said.

"Lauren," she replied, also shaking hands.

"Well, Doctor and Doctor, this is what's commonly called a production number. They're here to see how a movie stunt is *really* made."

"Don't they already know that?" Lauren asked.

"Sure," Piper explained. "This is a spectacle, a do-over. We don't see these very often."

"Nothing bad's likely to happen, right?"

Lauren questioned, her eyes opening a little wider.

"No," Piper said before either Cal or Tamara could jump in to reply.

Piper knew how both Tamara and Cal felt about her doing the stunt. They were worried about her. While Piper had some apprehension, she also had confidence in herself and in the people she worked with.

"We'll be ready by eleven." Piper reminded them of the time. All the conditions they could duplicate would come together at eleven in the morning. It was barely nine now, but the place was set up. Cameras were trained on every inch of the framework, both inside and out.

Her comment acted as a sign that it was time to break up. They cleared the table and left for Piper's ranch. She wanted to go over it one more time. She and Cal walked the property. He took measurements every now and then. Looking up, they noticed camera operators on the roof. High-powered cameras were mounted on various scaffolds waiting for their controllers to begin rolling them. A series of steel poles that shot up toward the sky held cameras on wires that would follow her progress.

"What are they doing up there?" Jake asked, pointing.

Piper looked in the direction he indicated. "They're going to film from up there."

"Apparently, they're filming from everywhere. I've never seen so many cameras," Lauren said.

Piper laughed. "Tamara has outdone herself. She must have called in every cameraperson she knows."

"And probably some she doesn't by the looks of it," Cal added.

Jake and Lauren looked at all the activity. "Do you mind if we just wander around?" Jake asked. "We've never been on a film set."

"Not at all. Just be careful of the wires on the ground."

"We will," Jake said.

His brother and sister-in-law walked toward one cluster of cameras.

Going back to checking things, Cal again started taking measurements of the platform.

"What are you doing?" Piper asked.

"Checking the temperature of the metal."

"That has to be something you can't do with a tape measure."

Opening his hand, she saw an instrument.

"It does the measuring and transmits the data directly to my computer." He touched the backpack he carried. "If there is the slightest variation, I want to know about it."

"You are very thorough," she said.

"Lives depend on it." His voice was calm, yet the seriousness of his words was heavily weighted.

Piper was sure Cal wished he could pull the words back the moment they were spoken.

But he couldn't.

A COMMOTION BEHIND them had Piper turning around. She closed her eyes against the scene she didn't want to have. If anyone could add more pressure to her day, he was walking toward her.

"This can't be happening," she whispered. "Not now. Not today."

"What's wrong?" Cal asked. Piper was squeezing his hand. She didn't remember taking hold of it. And she was unaware of the pressure her fingers were exerting on his hand.

Piper sighed before speaking. "The man coming up the hill," she said, staring at him. "That's Xavier Fabriano."

He had his head down due to the steep grade of the land, but he'd obviously been told exactly where she was. His gait as he made his way toward her was determined despite the pitch of the hill.

Piper felt bile rise in her throat. She pushed it down. How could she have ever thought she was in love with him? He looked like a small man now. Not in height. He was six feet tall and had all the charm needed when he decided to turn it on, but in terms of his character. The way he'd treated her was unconscionable.

Cal moved closer to her. She'd let go of his hand and stepped forward.

"Take a deep breath," he whispered into her ear.

She did.

"Blow it out slowly."

Again, Piper complied. "He called me awhile back. Woke me up. This will be the second time I'll have to deal with him over this stunt."

"I'm here. You're not alone," Cal told her. Piper glanced at him, grateful for his support.

Before Cal could say anything further, Xavier was in front of them. For a moment he said nothing. He was out of breath and took time to calm himself.

"Hello, Xavier, I didn't expect you'd quit your busy schedule to come here."

"You're going to kill yourself," he blurted out.

"I don't think so. We've practiced this several times over."

He looked up at the framework, shielding his eyes from the sun. "You've set it up wrong. And I won't be responsible for that."

"Why would you?" Piper asked. "You canned me. Our contract has been rendered null and void. In fact, since this is my property, you are trespassing. I did not invite you here."

"Have you checked the regulations?"

He ignored her comment.

"Is it even legal for you to perform this here?" Xavier gestured toward the apparatus.

"We've complied with all the laws and regulations," Cal said, coming to stand beside her. "We filled out all the paperwork and got the required permission."

"Who are you?" Xavier demanded.

"I'm the engineer who oversaw the design and construction of this." He waved his hand, indicating all the scaffolding and cranes that were in place. "I've done the math a hundred times over. I've calculated Piper's mass and weight. The clothes she'll wear, even the traction of her running shoes. I know the height of the scaffolding, each arm's distance to the ground, the size of the poles she's going to have to catch and climb over, the wind shear, heat index and all the known factors for this stunt. We're leaving nothing to chance."

"Well, I've set up hundreds of stunts and I tell you this one won't work. Piper may as well pull it down. She knows. She's assembled it before and the outcome wasn't pretty."

"When Piper designed it back in Hollywood and you were the coordinator, why didn't you tell her it wouldn't work then?"

The color dropped from Xavier's face. His speech sputtered before he regained both his anger and his speaking ability.

"She wanted a chance to do her own setup, so I gave her the opportunity and look what happened. We had a man fighting for his life after everything went haywire."

"That's why we're staging this today," Piper said. "No one could actually tell what happened and Austin doesn't remember."

"You're going to risk yourself to find out?" Xavier threw at her.

"Of course, I'm not. But I need to know what, if anything, went wrong."

"You know what went wrong," he said.

Cal was ready to intervene. Piper could feel it. The crew had stopped what they were doing and were now watching them.

"I know what *you* said went wrong. But I don't believe you. You were so quick to assign blame to me, and that may be warranted, but I will only know the truth if I re-create it. And that's what I'm going to do."

"You never were one to listen to reason," he said. "And all to prove you were right. But, believe me, you're wrong."

Then, like any movie actor delivering a parting shot, Xavier turned and exited stage left.

"I would laugh," Cal said. "If I didn't want to grab the guy and punch his lights out."

CHAPTER TEN

PIPER LOOKED AT Cal for a second. His words came back to her, comforting her. *I'm here. You're not alone*, he'd said. Not like Xavier had done in a similar situation. He'd blamed her, thrown her to the proverbial wolves. Not Cal. She knew he'd stand by her no matter the outcome. They were partners. Every step of this project they'd worked hand in hand, complementing each other, filling in for each other when there was a gap.

She trusted him. If he said everything was fine, then it was. They'd gone over hundreds of computer scenarios and the stunt *should* work. She had to say should because nothing was foolproof.

Piper watched as Xavier walked away.

"He's certainly a character," Cal said.

"That sums him up more than you know." She laughed a little, but she didn't really feel any humor. The day had arrived and there was no going back now, not if she truly wanted to know what had caused the accident.

"I'd better go change now," she told Cal.

He smiled and squeezed her hand as she started toward the house. It didn't take long for her to put on the green outfit. It was exactly like the one that Austin had worn, a jumpsuit fitted to her form. Her hair was pinned up and her face clean of makeup. There were no loose sleeves or pant legs, hazards that could catch on anything. Her shoes were soft-soled sneakers that closed with Velcro strips instead of laces.

Checking the bedside clock, it was close to the appointed time. Piper took a deep breath and dropped her shoulders. For a moment, she closed her eyes and rolled her neck, relaxing as she envisioned the task ahead.

When she reached the porch steps, Xavier made another appearance. He'd obviously been waiting for her. She wondered who'd told him she was doing the stunt today and why he'd traveled all the way from Los Angeles to try and stop her.

"I've looked over the equipment," he began.

"And I'm going to injure myself, right?" She knew the rhetoric as if it was a script.

"Right. I know what you're planning and nobody can do that. Not since the Hitchcock era has anyone done a stunt this way." Xavier referred to one continuous long scene that went from shot to shot without a break to reset lighting and camera angles.

"It doesn't matter. I knew you wouldn't approve. How did you know about this anyway?"

"The word is out all over town."

"Town being Hollywood?"

"There are no secrets in the movies." He smiled.

"This isn't Hollywood." She paused a moment. "I'm surprised you're here. Hollywood isn't the other side of the world, but it's a long way from Montana."

"I'm here trying to keep you alive." Xavier's voice was low, yet it held a note of strength she was all too familiar with.

"And why is my welfare of concern? You were quite willing to watch me go to jail for years when last we met."

"That's not true. I knew you'd be exonerated."

"So it was fine for you to tell the authorities that you had nothing to do with the planning and execution of the stunt? When you finished telling the tale, it was unclear whether you even had a company involved in the movies at all."

"That's not true—"

"It's absolutely true," she interrupted him. "Now, I'm on my way to do this stunt. You can go or stay. I have no idea who let you know this was happening today, but it *is* happening."

She moved to go to her set place.

"If you really want to know, I got a call."

He stopped, using all the mechanics of the pregnant pause. Piper continued walking.

"It was Caleb Masters," he called.

Piper stopped as if she'd hit an invisible wall. Slowly, she turned around. Xavier was leaning against the steps, a smug look on his face.

"Cal? Cal called you?"

He nodded.

Abruptly, she turned and headed for Cal. He was talking to Tamara when he saw her coming. Stepping away, he headed for her.

He had to know something was wrong. Piper did nothing to curb her confusion.

"You called him?" she accused. "You called Xavier and invited him here?"

Cal looked taken aback. "I can explain."

"Why?" Piper asked the question, but she didn't give him time to answer. "Didn't you think I'd be nervous enough doing this without having my ex-fiancé and the man who accused me of bungling the stunt the first time in the audience?"

"Piper—"

"I thought you were on my side," she continued. "I should have known."

She saw his shock and hurt. Piper didn't care. She'd trusted him. It was only a few minutes ago that she was telling herself how much she trusted him. How many times did she have to go through it before she committed it to long-term memory? Hurrying, she strode away, determined not to let him see her emotions.

Cal called her name, but she ignored him.

Piper reached the director, ready for her challenge. "I'm all set," she said.

"No, she's not," Cal countered. "We need to talk."

"I have a stunt to do," she countered.

"Not in this state. We're going to talk, alone or with an audience. Your choice."

Piper had had enough stories spread about her. She didn't want to provide more fodder to the folks watching her.

"All right," she said. "You've got five minutes and not a second longer."

CAL GLANCED AT the crowd. All eyes were on them. Convincing Piper to follow him to the other side of the metal structure, they retreated into their small temporary office.

"He had to be here. Don't you see that?" Cal said as soon as the door closed and before Piper could speak.

"No, I don't." She folded her arms. "You didn't think I had enough pressure on me?" Disappointment pushed her on. "This is a stunt where a man almost died. Yes, I feel like I did everything right and I'm about to find out. There are a hundred people out there, some of them waiting for me to fail. Despite Xavier trying to get me to cancel, he's one of them."

Piper sucked in a long breath.

"I thought he was the one you were trying to prove yourself to," Cal explained.

"Prove myself?"

"Prove yourself," Cal repeated, his voice a beat stronger. "He's been here with you for over a year. Everything you do has him as the object. You talk about wanting to redo this stunt. You've spent hundreds of hours looking at the video, re-creating this." He waved his hand to indicate the yard. "This is all so you could prove you were right and that he was wrong."

"I have not."

"You've been doing it so long, you don't even realize that's the point," he told her.

"You're wrong," she contradicted.

Cal watched her face pale.

He moved toward her. She held her ground. "It's the truth. And you know it. You don't want word to get back to him that your stunt was a success. You want the satisfaction of knowing that he was *here* to bear witness." He paused, giving her a chance to deny it.

She didn't.

"You should want him here. To close a wound that's been left open ever since the accident happened."

"I couldn't care less—"

"Stop," Cal insisted. "Be honest with yourself. You've been waiting for this day. And I wasn't the only one who let him know that the stunt was going down today."

Piper looked stunned. She didn't have to ask who. With the way she tilted her head toward the group outside, it was apparent that Tamara had also made a call. Cal didn't know who else, but he suspected several of the crew had also done what he had.

"You're right," Piper said. Her voice was so low, Cal wasn't sure he heard her.

"I am." It wasn't a question.

"I have been wanting to prove that I was right," Piper admitted. "And I did want Xavier to know it. When he called me, I didn't tell him to come, but I let him know I wouldn't back down."

"So, am I forgiven?"

Piper looked at him hard. He wanted her forgiveness. He wanted to make sure he'd come to the right conclusion. As much as he disliked Xavier, he knew she needed him here. And he also wanted to make sure there was nothing left between them that could affect her concentration.

"I guess I'll have to forgive you. You were right. I admit that. In a few minutes, I might have to eat crow if I'm proved wrong, that I didn't do something I should have and a man was hurt."

"You did everything right," Cal assured her.

He watched as she searched his face, probably for a sign of insincerity. Finally, she smiled and he relaxed.

"One more thing," Cal said. "Neither Tamara nor I called Xavier. He called us."

HE'D CALLED CAL. "Xavier called you?" Piper was more than confused. She was stunned. "He said you called him."

"He called the ranch and I was there. Naomi answered the phone and pried Xavier's name out of him before she'd give him any information."

"Why?" She was stumped. "Why did he call you?"

Cal shrugged. "I don't know. With all these California people coming to Waymon Valley, it wouldn't be hard to find out what was going on and where to find a local number."

"And then there's Tamara. You said he spoke to her, too."

"Technically, she still works for him. I'm sure he had a way of getting in touch, obviously."

"What did he say?" Piper was still trying to wrap her brain around the fact that Xavier had called and that he was on the property. It was out of character for him.

"He only asked when the stunt was taking place. I answered and he hung up."

"Why didn't you tell me?"

"I didn't want to add another worry to your list. But it seems that was a fruitless pursuit, since the outcome was the same."

"Well, he's here now and I'll do this routine with or without his presence." Piper was adamant.

"That's my Piper," Cal said, backing her up.

"Don't go that far," she said. "I'm still angry with you for not telling me you two spoke and that he knew today was the day."

Outside again, Piper tried to push her doubts aside. Returning to climb the scaffolding, she eyed the huge beast. It felt larger than it had a moment ago. Time and doubt seemed to make it grow.

"It's time," she told Cal. "I feel like I won't fail."

She took a step toward the metal structure. Strong hands took her arms and turned her around.

"That's exactly the way it is." Cal's face was close to hers, his voice strong and convincing. "You won't fail in this attempt. You are not going to suffer that fate."

He pulled her into his arms and kissed her. Kissed her hard. Piper hadn't expected that. She knew Cal was on her side, that he believed in her. The two had avoided getting even closer because their time in Montana was limited. If this stunt went as planned, she'd be exonerated. She could go back to Hollywood and resume her career.

And Caleb Masters could resume his.

But his arms were around her now, sure in their strength. She'd been stiff from the surprise, but just as quickly she relaxed. Soon, Cal stopped the kiss and stepped back, his head bowed as he stared at the ground.

"I've been wanting to do that for weeks," he said, looking up at her.

"Well, you picked a fine time for it," she said, attempting levity that didn't work. Not for her and not for him. Her voice was too breathy, her emotions too close to the surface. "Getting back to you will be on the top of my mind while I'm up there." She nodded toward the iron skeleton.

"Don't," he warned her. "Concentrate on every step. We've done this. It's going to work. But you need to be focused. Nothing should come between you and the perfect execution of each step."

She nodded, unable to speak. The intensity of his voice reached inside her and wrapped itself around her core. After one long look, she pushed his arms aside, raised herself up on her toes and kissed him as hard as he'd kissed her.

If this stunt went wrong, she wanted to make sure she knew once and for all what it was like to feel his mouth on hers. Piper had thought about it more than once. Yet it was nothing like she could imagine.

It was so much better.

LEAVING CAL BEHIND, but taking the kiss and its effects with her, Piper stopped as Tamara approached.

"Take a deep breath," Tamara said. "I just saw what happened."

Closing her eyes, Piper did as instructed.

"How do you feel?" she asked.

Fine. The automatic response was on her lips, but she didn't say it. She knew Tamara's question had nothing to do with the stunt. She wanted to know about the kiss. "Confused," she finally said.

"Take another breath. And imagine the stunt. Go through it from start to finish." It was a technique they often applied before the cameras started rolling.

"I've heard this speech before," Piper said. She knew Tamara wanted her to think of nothing except executing the stunt precisely and efficiently.

"Quiet. Just do what I said."

Piper did, and a few minutes later, she was ready. She nodded at the other woman, a signal they both knew.

Piper climbed into the harness. From the corner of her eye, she saw Xavier coming. She braced for another argument. Cal intercepted him, arguing with Xavier and barring him from coming any farther. She smiled, thinking both of Cal's aid and Tamara's directions. Piper no longer had Xavier in her head. She turned to the structure. It wasn't the monster she'd seen from her kitchen window. It was a prop, an apparatus that had no life and no consciousness. It did not lead or impede her. And she was prepared to go through it.

"I'm ready," she said with confidence.

"Break a leg," Tamara said with a confident smile. She backed away as did the crew who weren't already in a stationary place. The camera crew started filming and the director called for action.

Piper took a deep breath without being told. She grabbed the first handle and swung into place. From here on, everything that happened was all on her. Here was her future, three minutes away.

CAL TENSED. He stepped away from Xavier and looked up at where Piper stood.

"If I hear a single sound from you, I'll bounce you off this property without blinking," he told the man. "She's been working on this for over a year and you'll do nothing to destroy her concentration or the proper outcome of this stunt."

The two men's eyes warred for several

seconds. Cal was determined not to back down. It didn't take long. Xavier brushed the air with his arm and walked away but took up a position where he could see everything.

Cal moved to stand next to Tamara. Though he was sure the stunt would work, all the science had told him it would, his mind was still racing.

"She's going to be fine," Tamara muttered.

Cal shifted his weight without thinking. He watched as Piper began her run. She was still on the ground, dodging various objects. Not realizing he was moving parallel with her as if he was mirroring the stunt. He held his breath. His heart pounded wildly. Piper swung around the handle she was holding and started her routine. She jumped into and then out of a Jeep and appeared to be running from someone. There was no one other than her in the sequence, although in the real film, she would be escaping from someone intent on harming her. Cal had never been on a movie set and was unaware of the acting ability of the participants. Piper's face showed the strain of her physical actions.

She glanced over her shoulder, checking for an assailant who wasn't there. The crew, like Cal, was silent, hardly breathing. She reached the first rung of the scaffolding and pulled herself up. Her footing was sure. "First threshold," he whispered under his breath.

Cal had seen her calisthenics, and he'd watched rehearsals, but he was awed at how lithe her body was, how quickly she moved and how sure she appeared. Her movements were almost ballet-like, her coordination flawless.

Her green bodysuit stood out against the backdrop of the sun and the gray metal. Her legs swung in the wind as she caught the bar above her head and appeared to lose her balance. Instinctively, the crowd gasped. Like a jungle cat with strong arms, she nimbly righted herself, regaining her balance and swinging her legs and arms in a practiced air dance. Her hair, loose now from the fitting she'd begun with, whipped around her face. She took no time to brush it aside. At the top of the scaffolding, she stopped and looked at the distance to the elevated galvanized steel walkway that was six feet wide and ten feet below.

Again, she checked over her shoulder.

Her expression showed an actor's fear. Cal wondered if all of that was acting or if it was real. It was real for him. His body was drenched in sweat.

Piper took a step back, then burst forward and jumped. She wore a tether to prevent her from falling to her death. Austin had worn one, too, he reminded himself. She was mimicking his steps in every way.

The jump was perfect. She landed on her mark.

Cal let out a breath as did the rest of the crew and spectators when her hands grabbed the solid bar and she swung her body through the latticework and into the cage. Here, she began another run. He heard her footsteps pounding on the metal bridge. He watched as the metal swung with the cadence of her stride. He was sure it was in unison with his heartbeat. The stunt was almost over. Just one last big jump. Cal stepped forward again, his head titled skyward, his hands shading his eyes. She was running into the sunlight, blinding now as it approached the noon hour.

Tamara took his arm, keeping him from moving any farther and in the line of one of the ground cameras. He stopped, still focused on Piper. The sun blinded him. For the split second Piper ran in front of it, he saw only her silhouette, then a flash of visibility before she popped out beyond the rays.

Her foot caught the cable as it was supposed to and she went over the edge, falling headfirst toward the ground. He watched, her arms flailing, her scream ear-piercing. Her body twisting in the air. She hit her mark on the air mattress dead on. The rubber gave against the momentum of her weight, taking the brunt of her and pushing against it to keep her safe.

She sat up victorious and pushed off the air cushion. Hands reached out to help her. The director shouted cut and the crew let out a collective breath. A second passed in total silence before the entire crowd applauded. Shouts of success cut through the air like a football stadium full of happy fans.

Cal was running toward her before he knew he'd moved. He remembered Tamara's hand on his arm, but no amount of pressure could keep him still after this.

He was there when she came off the mat. She reached for him and Cal let go of all logic and restraint, pulling her to him and hugging her as if his life depended on their making contact.

"IT WORKED," she shouted, her grin wide. Cal pushed her slightly back, then lifted her, swinging her off the ground and around in a full circle. Piper was thrilled with relief and impulsively wanted to share it with Cal. She longed to kiss him, but the crowd surged then and she was pulled away. People shouted, called her name, congratulated her. At times the sound was so loud, she couldn't hear anyone distinctly. Searching for Cal, she saw him at the edge of the gathering. While the action around him swayed and moved, Cal remained in one spot. Austin stood next to him.

"Austin," she cried, trying to get his attention. Pushing against the flow of bodies, she headed for the scene's original stuntman.

Another wave of applause went up when she reached the former stuntman and pulled him into a tight hug. "You made it," she said.

Pushing her back, he looked at Piper. "I wouldn't miss it. You did good, Piper. It was almost perfect," he said.

"Almost?" Cal questioned.

Austin glanced at him, then at Piper. "You missed the bag."

"Bag? What bag?" she asked, a frown marring her face.

"I remember it now," he said. His face held an expression of surprise, as if the thought had just come to him.

"On the day of the shoot, one of the metal girders was loose. It was time for the stunt. Xavier jumped on it and said it was solid enough."

"I wondered what he was doing up there," Piper muttered as she remembered the moment. Xavier often inspected a stunt, but he rarely went up on anything high. He wasn't afraid of heights, but he left them to the construction crew.

"Go on," Cal prompted. "What about this bag?"

"He put a sandbag against the girder so there wouldn't be a loose strut. I remember Xavier telling me to jump over it when I got to that point. But I tripped on it. I forgot it was there, and since I had to look back, my foot hit it and that threw me off."

"Let me get this straight," Tamara said.

"Instead of calling someone from construction to fix the girder, Xavier covered it with a sandbag?"

"That's right. You can ask Xavier." He looked up and all eyes followed his gaze.

"So, Piper did nothing wrong," Tamara stated.

"Not that I can recall. The stunt was perfect. It was my fault I didn't tell you sooner. If I'd remembered that sandbag, it would have gone off without a hitch."

Piper stared at him for a long moment. Then she took off, walking determinedly toward Xavier, who was heading for his rental car. Tamara wasn't far behind her with Cal and a group of others bringing up the rear.

"What's she going to do?" Cal asked no one in particular.

"My guess," Austin said. "Is she'll read Xavier the riot act. What he did isn't against any rules, but his handling of the situation, and definitely the aftermath, foisting the blame on Piper's design and lying at the investigation, could cost him his license and his business. No one will hire him again."

"I take it Piper is going to make sure the record is set right. Let people know the truth," Cal said.

"She won't have to." Austin looked around.

Cal followed his gaze. Cameras were everywhere and they were trained on the small group in the temporary parking area. Piper was confronting Xavier and he looked mad.

"At least a dozen people heard my statement," Austin said. "I'll have to go to the authorities and tell them what I remember. It might go against me, too. I knew the bag was there and technically I consented to it. But I didn't know the blame would go to Piper."

Cal thanked Austin and joined the group in the parking lot.

"You have to understand, Piper—" Xavier was saying.

"I do not," she said fiercely, cutting him off. "You railed against me, dragged me through the mud. You tarnished my reputation. You even told the authorities that the accident was caused by me. My negligence. When the truth is, it was *you*. It was your negligence. And lies." She took a deep breath. Tamara squeezed her hand, presumably to let her know she had allies all around her. "Well, the record will be put straight," she said.

"There's nothing you can do," Xavier told her.

"I won't have to." She turned around and opened her arms.

Xavier must have forgotten the multitude of cameras pointed toward them. There were also media people. Many had been notified by Tamara. The entire episode was recorded and would be reported on every medium from entertainment shows to traditional print newspapers. Xavier's pallor went from beet red to snow white. Cal wasn't sure the man would be able to stand much longer with so much blood draining from his brain.

"I'm sure with the internet and social media, word will reach Hollywood before we can walk back to the house," Piper said.

"It looks like your days as a stunt coordinator are numbered," Tamara said.

"Don't worry. I'll survive," Xavier said. Slipping behind the wheel of his rented car, he turned the engine on. The crowd parted. Spitting dirt and gravel behind him, Xavier drove away.

Cal slipped his arm around Piper's waist.

He was proud of her. She stepped closer to him, her own arm snaking about his waist. He loved the moment so much he could have stayed that way for the rest of his life.

CHAPTER ELEVEN

PIPER'S FEET WERE back on solid ground thanks to Lauren. She'd guided Piper into the house for a short rest and much-needed hydration. Despite Piper's happiness, the tension of the day was sapping her of energy. Dr. Masters recognized it and got Piper away from the many well-wishers who all seemed to need to talk to her.

An hour later, dressed in a soft plaid shirt, jeans and boots, Piper prepared to go back outside.

"Thanks, Lauren," she said and squeezed Lauren's hand.

Cal's sister-in-law smiled and handed her a bottle of water. Piper was more grateful for her than she knew. Lauren rejoined her husband and the two celebrated with the crowd. Piper envied them. Would she ever find a love like they had?

She had no time to think about that question. Someone called her name and she was distracted. It really was true, Piper thought. She felt lighter since the weight of the past two years had been removed from her shoulders. The scene in the yard could only be described as a well-deserved party. Food, music and countless friends, neighbors and coworkers congregated like a huge family picnic. Piper lost track of the number of times someone stopped her to say congratulations.

She was back.

People knew she had nothing to do with the accident, that it was caused by Xavier. While Austin had known there was danger in the attempt, he had no complicity in ruining her career. He'd accepted Xavier's assessment of the situation on the day.

Xavier must have felt relieved when Austin woke up with no memory of the incident. If Cal hadn't suggested she re-create the accident, and if Austin hadn't shown up, the truth might have been hidden forever.

"Come on, people. It's a celebration," Tamara shouted to the gang.

The group cheered, renewing the festivities. They moved back toward the food. Cal had his arm around her. Eventually they were pulled apart as more people hugged her, saying they always believed in her and knew she had nothing to do with the accident. She accepted their comments as she looked at Cal happily. His eyes held something like longing. Quickly, it was gone. Piper wondered if she had imagined it. Had she put it there because she wanted to see it?

She didn't have time to ponder. From somewhere behind her, music started and in an instant she was whirled around for a dance. Food and drinks flowed and Piper had no idea where all the fun came from, but she was sure Ally, Naomi and Meghan had something to do with it. At the end of the dance, she saw Ally, the diner owner, beelining for the food. Piper waved at the three women. She intended to say thank you but was waylaid by a stuntman she used to work with.

"I've seen some pretty determined people in my time," he said. "But, Piper, you got chutzpah."

Piper smiled as someone else called her name and she looked up. She lost track of Cal.

"If you ever want to do something like this again, count me in," the man said.

She left him with a wide smile on his face. It seemed every stunt company manager there wanted to talk to her. As soon as she tried to stand in one place, someone else came up to her and tried to get a few words in. She was invited back to Hollywood to discuss working on various films by more than one director. She didn't commit but also didn't turn anyone down.

It was a whirlwind of conversations and Piper tried to keep a perspective on things. She also kept looking for Cal. When she spotted him, he was across the yard and not looking her way. Eventually she saw him talking to one of the stunt coordinators. Several others joined the conversation and there was laughter all around. She made a mental note to ask him about it later. Piper wanted to get his attention, smile at him, let him know that he was integral to her success. Despite all the people congratulating her, Cal deserved the same accolades. Without him, today wouldn't have happened.

Yet he never turned toward her.

The party went on and eventually Piper settled into it. She moved like a hostess, speaking to everyone and making sure they had what they needed while still trying not to commit to anything. She needed time to think. Today had given her several opportunities for her career, but she knew it was too soon to make any decisions.

After a while, the group thinned out and Piper had a moment to sit down. She couldn't pinpoint when the group began doing stunts, but whenever a group of performers got together, they performed.

"Piper, help me show them how we did the fight scene in *Red Dress Diaries*," veteran stuntman Lou Post said.

"This is the choir." Piper looked around, encompassing the yard with her arm. "They already know how."

"We don't," Jake spoke up.

Piper's attention was drawn to Jake and Lauren.

"Ditto for me," one of the camera operators chimed in. "I'm a student and I'd like to see it."

The crowd urged her on, and after a moment, she stood up. The stunt was supposed to be Elisabeth Grey in her role as Jane Treeloft. She was being chased by the villain. Cornered, she had to turn and fight for her life. She and her adversary moved in a circle a couple of times, taunting each other. Even today without the director, it was like a choreographed dance.

"This is going to be fun," Lou said, the same as he'd done when they were on the set. Then he attacked. Piper blocked him, using her agile skill and lower center of gravity to get behind him. Through several kicks that neither connected nor hurt, but looked real to a viewing audience, the practiced routine played out. Applause followed and she and Lou took their bows.

It was entertaining. Several others re-created past stunts until the sun began to set and people started saying good-night. Piper smiled at them, said good-night and agreed to keep in touch. All the while she was concerned about Cal. He didn't seem himself, at least not after the stunt was over. He smiled and responded in all the right places, but she could tell something just wasn't right. She wondered if Jake saw it, too. From the way he looked at his brother, she felt a vibe of concern within the doctor.

Was Cal thinking what she was thinking? Despite her merriment, the smiles and laughter that came from her, she wasn't at heart an actress, but her bout with reporters and cameras had taught her to keep her expression calm and neutral when she could. For a long while, she'd been using that learned method even in her private life.

She knew her time with Cal was over. The daily contact they'd had up until today was at an end. The goal they'd worked so hard for was realized. She looked at the skeleton of the stunt. The huge structure still reached for the sky, even in the dark. It was over, successful, yet it all seemed to be saying goodbye.

She hadn't spoken to Cal in a while. Looking over the dwindling crowd, she still didn't see him. She hadn't seen him in at least an hour. Where had he gone? Didn't he want to celebrate with her? Piper didn't have to ask herself that question. He'd kissed her before the stunt and she knew he wanted to be with her. Had he changed his mind? Was his kiss just an act? Piper dismissed the notion. She didn't think so.

Making her way to the food tables, where things were being broken down, she approached Naomi. "Have you seen Cal?" she asked.

She was in the process of transferring left-over pasta from a huge pan to a smaller container. She didn't look at Piper but spoke over her shoulder. "I think he went back to the house with the two doctors."

"House?" Piper whispered to herself. "Thanks," she said. Then remembering her gratitude, she turned back.

"Naomi, thanks for all you, Meghan and Ally did for the crew and me. I know everyone appreciated it."

Naomi smiled. "Just wait till you get the bill." The older woman winked. For Naomi, that was a compliment.

Looking over, Piper stared toward Cal's ranch. It was impossible to see from where she stood on this side of the hill. If she'd been on the scaffolding, the house would be visible. Had Cal gone home? Maybe. She no longer saw Jake or Lauren. He hadn't said good-night. She and Cal had worked together for so long, they each knew what the other would say. They'd said good-night for weeks and they never parted without saying something. How could he leave like that? She felt lost without him.

The last time she'd seen him, he was talking to Rance Wilson, a highly sought-after stunt coordinator. He'd spoken to several other coordinators, too. Piper thought they might just be interested in how she and Cal came to redesigning and pulling off today's epic.

By the time everything was put away for the night, and the last guests had departed, Cal had not appeared. Piper flirted with the idea of going to his ranch, but discarded it. It was late and she was exhausted from both the physical activities and the drama that preceded it. Pulling her phone out, she punched in Cal's number. The call went straight to voice mail. She listened to his strong voice. At least she had that.

PIPER WAS GOING to miss that monstrosity when it was gone. The huge skeleton looked back at her as if it was angry that she had conquered it. Standing on the porch the following evening, she looked out on the remains of the day. The sun was setting and the day had been long. She had several students, all with questions about the stunt. Apparently, the stories in town had been amplified, and since they were children without filters, they gave her several versions of what the day before had been like. Thankfully, they only talked about the stunt and not the aftermath of her confrontation with Xavier.

For years she'd thought about him and the accident. For weeks she and Cal had worked on re-creating the stunt that resulted in it. She already missed the crew that had tirelessly built the structure and Tamara's direction of the entire complex web of details. The huge amount of people that contributed had all gone back to their usual lives. Except for Tamara, who was leaving in a couple of days, Piper was alone.

Now it was over.

She should feel elated. She had for a while last night, but the little bit of revenge she got against Xavier wasn't as sweet as she thought it would be. She'd set out to prove herself right. Or as Cal said, to prove Xavier wrong. Both things happened.

And now the carnival was over. Outside, she strolled along the porch and claimed a chair. Only the debris spreading across the lawn and the massive skeleton were left as reminders of the frenzy that had occurred just twenty-four hours ago. Soon a cleanup team would come to clear the last remnants away, leaving only the memories of her time working with Cal.

"Reflections?"

Piper almost jumped at the sound. Looking to her left, she saw Cal leaning against the porch post. Her heart thumped. "I can't help but think about how the day went."

"It went amazingly. It's been a long few months in the making," he said.

Longer than he knew, she thought. And in the coming months, she was sure they would be longer than any that had come before.

Pushing away from the porch post, he lowered himself into the chair next to hers.

"Soon it'll all be over," Piper said.

"All but the monster out there." Both Piper and Cal glanced at the steel structure.

"What are you going to do with it?" he asked.

They had talked about building the skeleton, the materials needed, how much it would cost, the labor, but never what would happen to it when all was said and done. Yet she had a solution.

"I spoke with one of the film schools. Actually, they approached me. I'm donating the apparatus, lock, stock and barrel."

"That's great," Cal said.

Again Piper thought how she would miss it when it was gone. It reminded her of all the time she and Cal had spent together. They did well as a team. She would miss that, too. And she'd miss him.

"I guess our collaboration is over, too," she said, looking out over the ranch and keeping her voice level.

"It was fun," Cal said, glancing at the metal structure. "Once I got over the fear that you'd hurt yourself."

She nodded. "I felt like the old me, that as long as I hit every beat on time, nothing would go wrong."

"I'm glad you were confident. My heart was working overtime until you finally came off that inflatable pad unscathed."

"Thanks for being concerned about me."

Cal met her eyes, then slightly turned his head. The sun was setting, so she couldn't see his expression, but she was almost sure she saw something there that he didn't want her to see. She felt as if he wanted to say something, but decided against it.

"You should get a lot of Hollywood offers now," he finally said.

The moment was lost.

"Yesterday, there was a ton of talk about your abilities, your gutsiness, your ability to cover all the bases and keep things safe."

"I saw you with a number of coordinators. They had just as many compliments about you."

Cal gave her a lopsided grin. "I enjoyed the last few months. It was like a new world, one where I used my knowledge and skills on something that was more personal."

"What do you mean?"

"I mean *you*."

Piper's heart did another flip.

"It was like this meant so much to you that I got caught up in it as if it was my project, too. I felt good about it."

"I know what you mean," she said. She felt the same. It was different because it was him, because she felt something for him. "By the way, what did Rance have to say? I saw you and him chatting."

"He spent a lot of time with me. One of the things was he wanted me to use my influence with you to get you to join his team."

Piper nodded. "He's got one of the best companies. I'll consider it." She'd had several offers pour in, but she hadn't committed to anything yet. She knew what was stopping her. Cal. He was the unknown. What about the two of them? Was there a them? Could there be a them?

"What will you do?" she asked. "Do you have plans to leave? Begin another engineering job somewhere in the world?"

Piper struggled to keep her voice normal. It almost cracked when she said *world*. He could be going anywhere. The ranch was an anchor. She could picture him there, even if she knew he'd left the Valley.

"I have a few things I'm considering."

A few, Piper thought. That was more than two. She knew Cal was a sought-after engineer. Her experience had told her he was efficient, methodical, and he took in all the angles to make sure the outcome was as planned.

His was a world where Piper didn't fit.

"What about you?" He broke into her thoughts. "I guess you'll have to decide soon if you're going back to stunt work in Hollywood or if you and Tamara are going to go into business together. You got both, exoneration and getting back to what you love doing."

"Yes," she agreed. "I got what I wanted." Her voice was flat. Piper understood the cliché of being careful of what you wish for. She wanted the truth to come out, but she knew there was always a cost to that. Her cost was that she and Cal were done. She'd fallen in love with him. It didn't matter that both of them weren't looking for a relationship. Cupid didn't take requests. The small cherub decided on its own who would be tapped to fall in love.

"So are you going to take one of those jobs or what about you and Tamara?"

"We haven't talked about joining forces yet. The knowledge is so new. This isn't the time to make decisions."

Piper hoped he'd understand that he shouldn't make any decisions at this time, either.

She stood up and leaned against the porch railing, facing Cal. "Seems like we all have decisions to make," she said.

Cal nodded. "Along these lines, I'm leaving tomorrow for an interview."

Piper was sorry she was facing him. She didn't want him to see her expression. Yet she didn't turn away. "How long will you be gone?"

"A couple of days. Three at the most."

"Interview?"

He answered with a nod.

He was already leaving, Piper thought. Whoever he was seeing would go out of their way to convince him to work for them.

She would.

She had to get used to being alone again. She would take one of those jobs in Hollywood. Maybe with Rance. The work would do her good. It would be without her running in and out of Cal's house and having Naomi fix her fried apples. It would be without a metal skeleton in her backyard. It wouldn't be dancing with him or riding a horse.

She wondered if he would think of her when he was somewhere under a full moon and she was inside a soundstage.

HE'S GONE. It was Piper's first thought when she woke the next morning. She might as well get used to it, she thought over her first cup of coffee. The excitement outside was history now and Piper sat enjoying a quiet moment alone.

It didn't take long before her solitude was broken by a slamming door and rushing feet.

"You'll never believe what's happened." Tamara practically danced with excitement. Her voice was high and her smile was larger than Piper had ever seen it. She carried an open bottle of champagne and two flutes.

"What are we celebrating?" Piper asked. "At nine o'clock in the morning?"

Taking a moment to make mimosas, Tamara poured them into the glass flutes. She handed one to a confused Piper, who accepted it.

"First to you and the successful stunt you pulled off." She waved her glass and danced around in a circle. "It was a kick in the gut to all the naysayers who mistakenly blamed you."

"They know the truth now," Piper said without malice. "And I didn't do it alone."

Tamara raised her glass in salute. "To success," she said. They both drank.

"What is the second thing?" Piper asked.

"Second!" Tamara paused dramatically, giving her a Cheshire cat grin. "To me." Again she raised her glass. "I'm going to be an actress." She pronounced it *awk-tress*.

"What?" Piper sputtered. She didn't drink or say anything further. She bounded up from the chair she was sitting in. "That's wonderful." For a moment she couldn't say anything else. Then she hugged her. They did a little circle around the room. Piper pushed back. "What happened? When did you decide this? I thought you wanted to start a stunt company."

"I do and I will, but Edmund King called me a few minutes ago. We had a long conversation. He said he liked my work on the screen and that he'd seen me in a few of those stand-in episodes I did under those emergency-we-need-an-actress roles. The bottom line is he wants me to play a role in his next movie, an on-screen role."

"I can't believe it," Piper said.

"Neither can I. I was floored."

Obviously, Tamara couldn't stand still. She moved back and forth as if her feet were on hot sand. "It was all I could do not to sink to the floor. Of course, I'll have to do a screen test."

Piper's melancholy was wiped away with the news. "You'll be great. I've seen you act. I've seen you play the main role while we were doing a stunt and the talent wasn't on the set. Thankfully, someone else recognized your ability."

"I'm to play a supporting role, the sister of the main character. And you'll never guess who the lead is."

"Tell me." Piper wasn't going to do the guessing game. Cal's leaving had been stressful and she was still reeling from Tamara's about-face. Besides, there were too many actresses for her to choose from.

"Anna Gavin."

Piper's mouth dropped open. Anna Gavin was the hottest property in Hollywood these days. Her box office receipts toppled all the records.

Piper screamed for joy. She hugged Tamara. For the second time, the two women jumped around the kitchen like two energetic thirteen-year-olds who'd just discovered they had dates with the hottest guys in school. "What a place to start."

"Speaking of starting, I have to go pack."

An hour later, Piper waved goodbye to her friend. She watched as Tamara drove her rented Jeep down the long driveway. Dust followed her. The place seemed even more lonely after she was gone. Despite Tamara's good news, which Piper was happy about, she felt as if she was in limbo. That nothing was solid. She'd proved herself. She had job offers, yet she didn't feel that anything was settled or would be settled.

Not until she accepted that she and Cal had no future. She was sure that when he returned, he'd let her know which job he'd accepted.

And that would be the end.

THREE DAYS AT the most, Cal had said when he left. Piper worked through her days as if she were on autopilot. She taught her lessons and fielded the phone calls that came in. Each time the phone rang, she hoped it would be Cal. But today, he should be back. Piper couldn't explain how happy she felt knowing she would see him.

She didn't take time for breakfast. Maybe Naomi would have some fried apples ready when she got there. Swinging her leg over Silver's saddle, she let the wind blow her hair back as she covered the distance between the two ranches.

Quickly tying the horse to the post, Piper knocked and opened the back door in almost one single movement. She was so used to just letting herself in that she didn't think to wait for permission.

Heading for the office, she was stopped by Naomi's voice.

"Missing him already?" Naomi asked.

"Cal isn't home?" Piper picked up on that. She stopped, turning around. "Where is he?"

"He didn't say."

"You talked to him?"

Naomi stopped working and looked her directly in the eye. "He left me a message saying not to fix breakfast."

"That's all?"

"You know he's a man of few words."

Emotion clogged Piper's throat. She was well aware of that. Since he left her porch three days ago, she hadn't heard one word from him.

"I suppose I'll go back to the ranch. I wanted to thank him again for all he did for me."

"Yeah."

The way Naomi said it, Piper knew the older woman understood that was not why she'd run into the kitchen and headed straight for Cal's office.

Pushing her hair back, Piper didn't respond to Naomi's comment. Naomi was always busy. She was unloading the dishwasher and putting things away. Since Cal hadn't been there in days, probably neither had Naomi. When Naomi left the room for a moment, Piper glanced at her phone. Quickly, she dialed Cal's number. It rang once and went straight to voice mail.

Waiting for the beep, she spoke even though who knew when he'd get the message. She wouldn't say anything about his interview. Softly, she said, "Good morning, Cal," and that was all she recorded, but she touched the phone as if she were brushing her hand over his.

Where was he? She entertained the thought of calling Jake and Lauren but decided against it. Naomi knew he was out of town. If a mishap occurred, Jake would let either her or Naomi know. No need to create problems where there were none.

The truth was she missed Cal. They needed to talk, but he apparently had fallen off the edge of the world.

She was still staring at the phone when Naomi returned.

"Sit down," Naomi said.

Piper did so and Naomi sat a breakfast plate in front of her as if she'd known Piper would come by. The fried apples she ladled on it reminded Piper of Cal. Everything these days reminded her of him.

"He didn't say where he was going?" Piper said again.

Naomi shook her head.

"He's interviewing," Piper said, more to herself than to Naomi. "He told me that before he left." Piper couldn't really blame him. He had to look out for his own life and career. They'd been focused on hers. She felt guilty for not thinking about what he would do after.

She'd tried to push him leaving to the back of her mind. That hadn't worked. Today, she was sure he'd be at the ranch. The two of them worked so well together. But Piper had done something she vowed to never do again. She hadn't thought of the future. She hadn't allowed herself to think beyond the stunt. She figured she could return to Hollywood, resume her career. But she hadn't thought of what Cal would do, how she'd feel about no longer seeing him, no longer being able to come and go in his house and office to discuss the project. The stunt was over. They had no reason to continue their routine.

But he'd kissed her and she'd kissed him. There was a promise there. At least it was for her and that was something they needed to talk about.

She was disappointed in herself. Her career wasn't the only one at stake here. Cal had a life, too. They'd agreed to not get involved, but her heart hadn't paid attention. She *was* involved. She was in love with Caleb Masters. She hadn't told him and she was unsure of his feelings. Yet their actions had spoken of something good. He'd kissed her. He had his arm around her waist as they walked together. That could have been part of the moment, part of the exalting energy of the day. How many times had she seen that in a movie? The couple fighting at the beginning, then working together and falling in love. For her, that had always been fantasy, the effort of some writer to manipulate the feelings of a movie audience.

How could she know it happened in real life?

The only difference was for her it didn't happen like it did on the screen. In this case, they completed the job they were doing together and immediately he flew off to start another project.

"You've fallen in love with him, haven't you?" Naomi interrupted her thoughts.

Piper's attention came back to the kitchen. Naomi was sitting in front of her with a cup of coffee. Piper hadn't seen her sit down, or even remembered that she was there. The breakfast plate in front of her was getting cold.

"Is it that obvious?"

"Only to an old girl like me." She smiled.

"Naomi, do you think he's coming back? I mean for more than to get his stuff and fly off again."

Piper heard the desperation in her own voice. Naomi reached across the table and took her hand.

"That's a question you'll have to ask him." Naomi looked Piper straight in the eye. "Before you do, be sure you want to hear the answer."

WHAT ANSWER DID she want? Piper asked herself that question as she slowly rode back to her house. Cal was gone, the crowds had returned to their homes and businesses. Her ranch reminded her of a ghost town. No noise, no activity, just the pressed grass that so many feet had crossed and recrossed. The empty metal skeleton rising monstrously toward the sky and the remnant of remembered noise seemed to mock her. Yet in all that quiet, she didn't hear Cal. What interview was he on and where in the world would it take him?

And why hadn't he called? Didn't cell phones work where he was?

The comment Naomi made stayed with her. Did she want him to say he was staying in Montana? She thought of the offers she'd had after the success of the stunt. She could write her own ticket, but it would mean going back to Hollywood and resuming her life there. Cal was probably already returning to his.

Was she too wrapped up in her own efforts that she hadn't thought about what might be shaping Cal's life? Piper knew the answer to that. She'd been singularly focused on herself. A wave of guilt accosted her as she thought of how he'd been there for her, yet she wasn't even interested enough to ask anything about what he would do.

And now he was gone. He'd taken her heart with him and he didn't even know it.

CHAPTER TWELVE

THE HOUSE SEEMED too quiet when Cal entered it. It was nearly midnight and Naomi was long gone. He assumed all the guests from the last few days were back in their own worlds. And Piper...

She was alone.

Grabbing a bottle of water from the refrigerator, he downed it facing Piper's ranch. A full moon hung in the sky, but Cal could still see the light on in her bedroom. He knew which of the rooms faced his ranch and he thought of her in that space whenever he saw it. Holding the empty bottle, he wondered why she was still awake. People in the Valley tended to go to bed with the sun and rise with it, too.

Cal knew he and Piper didn't adhere to those rules. They'd been together day and night for months. He wanted to talk to her. It was how he'd spent much of his time and he missed that now. He wanted the noise of her clicking keys on her computer or the sound of her watching the video of the accident and their own construction of the framework that she ran through.

But the only thing present now was the sound of his breathing or his footsteps as he ambled through the empty rooms.

The light in her upstairs bedroom went out. She was probably going to sleep. Then a few moments later, a light went on downstairs. He could barely see it because of the rise in the land. For a moment, he wondered if he was wishing it on. Pulling his cell phone from his pocket, he checked the phone log. Several calls from her popped up on his display.

He smiled, hoping they meant she'd missed him. He'd missed her, but she had a decision to make and he didn't want to influence her. He had one to make, too, but it depended on several things happening.

Typing carefully, he sent her a text. Are you awake?

Yes was the rapid reply.

Can we talk?

Yes came again.

I'll be right there.

Cal's spirits along with his heartbeat rose. He felt light on his feet, wanting to get to see her, confirm the mental image he carried with him all the time. Passing through the kitchen, he spied the cake Naomi always seemed to have under a dome on a glass pedestal. He cut two slices and in seconds was in his truck, racing over the ground he'd driven hundreds of times in the past months. The dust cloud behind him was visible in the rearview mirror. Stopping in front of the house, he was out of the truck the moment he shifted it into Park.

Piper appeared on the porch. He expected her to be wearing a robe over pajamas, but she was fully dressed in jeans and a long sweater. It took all his energy not to rush forward and pull her into his arms. He'd missed her, missed her red hair highlighted in the sun, missed her smiling face and bright eyes, missed seeing her day in and day out. Still, he took the steps two at a time. They faced each other. Neither spoke for a moment. Cal felt awkward. He wanted to see her, had rushed to get to her. Now he was searching for words.

"I brought you a dessert." He pulled the two slices now meshed together inside a plastic container. "It's what people used to do to be friendly. I'm not sure if that's still the truth, but I was taught that way." He repeated the words he'd said to her months ago when he first stepped on her porch.

She smiled widely, trying not to laugh. Getting control of herself, she said, "I don't eat a lot of carbs." Her response was the same as she'd given him at their first meeting. "Where did you go?" Piper asked, changing the subject.

"After I left you?" he asked.

They had been on this very porch.

"I called several times, but you didn't answer."

"It was your night, Piper. You were in the world you know. The one you love and want to return to. All the people who like and respect you were here. They all wanted your attention. And you deserved the limelight. You deserved some time to think things through, decide what you want."

"So you were giving me time by not returning my calls?"

She moved to the edge of the porch and looked out into the darkness that a few days ago had been teeming with people.

"Not exactly," Cal told her. He went to stand next to her. "My first flight was to Qatar."

"They have cell phones there."

"True, but at a petroleum facility, they are strictly forbidden. I wanted to call, but I couldn't. When I could, it was the middle of the night here."

"Not even when you touched down in the States?" she asked.

Cal knew she was right. He felt guilty.

"We'd talked so much before the stunt," Piper continued. "After it was over, I wanted to discuss it with you." She stopped, but before he could respond, she went on. "I realize I'd taken a lot of your time over the last few months and that you had to take care of your career. Did any of your interviews prove successful?"

"I want to answer that after I ask you a question."

Her eyes opened wider and he almost reached for her then.

"What?" she said.

"You mentioned you had several offers to return to stunt work. I wanted you to be free to accept one or more of them. If that's what you really wanted."

It was what she wanted and what they had worked toward. Cal looked at the framework in the distance. It was still standing. In the dark, silhouetted in the moonlight, it looked ominous. "The two of us spent hundreds of hours working on the stunt. Now it's over."

This day had to come. Cal knew it. Why did he feel like he was losing something? He'd never felt that way before. Once a job was complete, there was the sense of accomplishment. What he felt now was a sense of loss. He and Piper had their own lives. He hadn't planned on staying in Montana. And after her stunt, neither was she. So why was he disappointed that she might be leaving, returning to a job she loved?

He didn't want her to go without him. Cal was in love with her.

"How many offers did you get?" Cal asked.

"Is that your question?"

He nodded.

"Five or six."

"Are you considering them?"

"I haven't ruled them out. I'm going to have to do something with the rest of my life and I've worked on stunts a long time. What about you? Did you accept one of yours?"

"Not yet."

"Are you going to?"

Cal felt her voice was a little high and he wondered if she was anticipating his reply.

"My answer depends on you."

"Me?" She leaned back against the porch railing. "What do I have to do with it?"

Cal reached for her hand. "My interview was for a job in Los Angeles."

"Oh?" She looked out on the mountains in the distance.

"Two choices," he said. "And they're on opposite sides of the world. My second meeting was with Rance Wilson."

"Really? Why?" She was clearly confused and impressed.

"He offered me a job as an engineer in his firm."

Hope lit her face, but it quickly faded. Her body tensed. "What did you say?"

"I turned it down."

Her face fell. "Rance runs the biggest and

best stunt firm in Hollywood. But…you're going to Qatar." It wasn't a question.

"I told him I was going to be working with a small start-up company."

"Start-up?" Piper repeated. "A small start-up in the Middle East wouldn't have flown you out there. You know Tamara's dream to start her own business, but…"

"It's not with her. And she's not starting it for a while."

"How did you know that?"

Cal laughed. "Not only was I in a meeting with Rance, but Edmund King, the director who wants Tamara for his movie, was also there. He's very enthusiastic about her. So Tamara will be busy for a while."

"She told me about postponing her business before she left," Piper said. "I'm thrilled for her. But if you're not going into a start-up with Tamara, who are you going into business with?"

Cal smoothed the lines on Piper's forehead.

"It's with you," he said.

For the first time, he thought she was speechless. "Me? I don't have a…" She stopped as his meaning dawned on her. Suddenly she was on her feet and hugging him. "You want to start a business with me?"

Cal hugged her back. For a long moment, he held her close, taking in her scent and never wanting it to go away. Finally, he released her.

"We work well together. We trust each other. You can do the design. I can manage the engineering, building what's necessary, and we can both do the safety checks. Eventually we can hire a crew full-time."

"Trust," Piper said. "I do trust you."

It appeared *trust* was the only word she'd latched on to.

Cal knew Piper was no longer talking about a business venture. Neither was he.

"I trust you, too," he whispered.

Suddenly, she pushed him away and stood back.

"What?" Cal asked.

"Do you really want to go into business with me? I mean your life in all those countries seems so exciting."

"And you don't think what you do is exciting?"

"I never really thought of it that way. It's very choreographed. But once the cameras start to roll, my heart is always up to here." She put her hand to her throat.

"I think we could work very well together. And I kinda like having roots somewhere."

Piper laid her head on his chest. "I've thought of something," she said.

"What's that?" Cal put his arm around her. There was nothing that could dissuade him to move from this spot.

"Tamara? When she begins her business…?"

"You don't have to worry about that. I spoke with her this afternoon. She's agreed to be a silent partner in our new venture. In fact, she was over the moon about it."

"That's a wonderful idea."

"From what I saw of her directing and overseeing multiple crews here, she'll be a great asset."

Piper tightened her arms around him.

"Now, for my one other thing," Cal said.

Piper looked up at him expectantly. "What is that?" She smiled.

"I know we said we weren't looking for a relationship. And with all that's happened, I want to be sure that we will work together because I've fallen in love with you." He said the last part quickly.

The smile on her face told him everything he needed to know. He scanned her features, checking every detail. Her eyes were shining, all trace of the sadness she'd worn for years was gone.

"I love you, too. I have for weeks now, but I was afraid to let you know."

Cal laughed heartily. "Now you tell me." Sobering, he said, "We don't ever need to be afraid to tell each other anything ever again."

He kissed her. This time it wasn't impulsive, like when they finished the stunt. This time it was real, not a movie, not a scene. It was love.

* * * * *

Get 4 FREE REWARDS!

We'll send you 2 FREE Books plus 2 FREE Mystery Gifts.

FREE
Value Over
$20

Both the **Love Inspired®** and **Love Inspired®** Suspense series feature compelling novels filled with inspirational romance, faith, forgiveness and hope.

THE NORA ROBERTS COLLECTION

Get to the heart of happily-ever-after in these Nora Roberts classics! Immerse yourself in the beauty of love by picking up this incredible collection written by, legendary author, Nora Roberts!

YES! Please send me the **Nora Roberts Collection**. Each book in this collection is 40% off the retail price! There are a total of 4 shipments in this collection. The shipments are yours for the low, members-only discount price of $23.96 U.S./$31.16 CDN. each, plus $1.99 U.S./$4.99 CDN. for shipping and handling. If I do not cancel, I will continue to receive four books a month for three more months. I'll pay just $23.96 U.S./$31.16 CDN., plus $1.99 U.S./$4.99 CDN. for shipping and handling per shipment.* I can always return a shipment and cancel at any time.

☐ 274 2595 ☐ 474 2595

Name (please print)

Address Apt. #

City State/Province Zip/Postal Code

Mail to the Harlequin Reader Service:
IN U.S.A.: P.O. Box 1341, Buffalo, NY 14240-8531
IN CANADA: P.O. Box 603, Fort Erie, Ontario L2A 5X3